DUPLICITOUS

TEFFETELLER MYART

Book Cover by Teffeteller Myart

Proofreader: Roxana Coumans

CONTENTS

Foreword

This book is a depiction of an abusive relationship, not a romantic ideal. Many of the aspects of BDSM depicted are incorrectly executed and are a form of abuse. Please heed warning, and always be safe.

This book also contains references to, and a brief scene of, child sexual abuse. Please use your discretion in reading this book.

There is an instance of sexual assault in this book as well (adult). Please use your discretion to determine if this book is for you.

1

Chapter One

Gloria Alexander-Titus woke alone—yet again—in her massive king size bed. She knew where she would find her husband, however...the same place she found him most mornings. Since they hadn't had sex the night before, of course he wasn't waking up beside her.

She hated how things were between them anymore. Not that they'd ever had the perfect relationship, much less the perfect marriage. When she'd found out she was pregnant soon after they became engaged—for the second time—he had been doting, worshiping the ground she walked on.

Pregnancy had been hard on Gloria, and he'd taken good care of her.

As soon as their baby was born—Genevieve Evangeline, Gloria's first baby ever, after longing to be a mother for her entire life—Henry had been happy, but even while she'd still been lying in the hospital bed, holding their newborn, he'd started talking about getting her pregnant again as soon as possible.

The delivery had been the single most terrifying experience of Gloria's thirty-two years. It had been painful, gory, and she was in desperate pain from her tear...the very thought of sex sounded like a nightmare.

Knowing that her husband had particular sexual tastes made Gloria more reluctant to think about him inside her already...she'd told him that he would have to wait six weeks before they could even *think* about being intimate, and even then, that he would have to be gentle, because she was seriously hurting.

He'd taken good care of her as she'd recovered, but he had never been a patient man.

That very night, as exhausted as she had been, with their baby sleeping in her crib beside their bed, he'd wanted her to suck him off.

And, stupidly, Gloria had...setting up the precedent that she would bend to his will, that she would put his needs above her own.

He only gave her two weeks before he asked her to allow him to have anal sex with her, saying that her rectum hadn't been torn, only her vagina. She'd still been swollen, and very sore, and anal sex hurt anyway, but again...she'd agreed.

"Thank you, babygirl," Henry had said that night, as Gloria positioned herself over his cock. She was nervous, not only because she knew he was going to hurt her, but also because Eva was asleep in her crib, and Gloria was terrified that their baby being in the room while her mother and father had sex would damage her psyche.

"Anything for you," she whispered, taking a shaky breath as she arched her back, preparing herself to be impaled by her husband's seven-inch cock.

He'd surprised her by taking her gently by her hips, stroking up and down her body, causing chill bumps to rise all over her smooth, soft skin. After a few moments, she realized he was trailing his fingers along her stretch marks, knowing how insecure she was about them.

"I love you, Gloria."

"I love you, too."

He grabbed the lube and rubbed it all over her asshole, easing his fingers inside her. "How does that feel, babygirl?"

"Um..."

He hesitated. "Gloria, if this isn't pleasant for you, I won't enjoy it, either."

"I know..."

He wrapped one hand around her neck, the other working through her hair, his fingers twisting through her long blond waves. He tugged gently, pulling her head back, so that she was looking into his eyes.

*He stared at her for a moment longer, then he softly smiled. "***Do** *you know, baby?"*

She swallowed. "I'm nervous."

"I can tell," he said, moving his hand that was wrapped around her neck down her back, to her ass, where he went back to teasing and gently stretching her asshole. "You're really clenching hard."

"Well, it hurts," Gloria whispered.

He kissed the side of her neck. "It won't hurt for long. You've just got to get used to me again."

He put some more lube onto his fingers, sliding three inside her. Gloria took a deep breath, doing her best to relax, to calm her nerves.

When he added a fourth finger, she whimpered in pain. "Um...baby. That doesn't feel good."

"Take a deep breath." He moaned, and she could tell that he was stroking himself now with the hand that wasn't shoved inside her asshole. "I'm so horny, Gloria."

Nervously, she sucked in another breath. "Well, maybe I should suck you off first, so that you're not too...so that I can take the edge off."

"You're really afraid of the pain, aren't you, babygirl?"

"Honestly? Yes," she said.

"So you don't want to have sex with me?"

She turned to face him. "Baby, I do, but I want to wait a little bit longer, until I'm healed up."

"Your ass ***is*** *healed."*

"Henry...I don't want you to hurt me."

"I won't hurt you."

She could tell that arguing with him was going to do no good. She could also sense his impatience, knowing that he was horny and that he got angry when he got horny...hangry in an entirely different sense.

"Okay," she said.

He cupped her face in his hand. "No, look at me, babygirl. Do you think that I would hurt you?"

She shook her head, biting her lip.

"I'm going to make sure that you're ready for me, and then I promised you that I would be gentle, didn't I?"

"Yes."

"Kiss me."

She turned her body so that she was kissing him, and he pulled her around to face him, when she'd intended to fuck him reverse cowgirl...that way, she would have been in control of how deep he went, and she could make sure that he didn't go too hard.

At least he was kissing her, holding her with some semblance of affection. Affection was what Gloria needed...despite all that she and Henry had gone through together in order to become husband and wife, she sometimes doubted his affection for her...as proven by the act they were engaged in.

As he kissed her, Henry rubbed her asshole with his lubed fingers, slipping them inside her, first his thick index finger, then his middle finger. Gloria whimpered, flinching at the stretch.

Henry placed his hand against her back, rubbing in gentle circles as he pulled his fingers apart.

"Henry..."

"What?" he asked, irritated.

"Um...I think it might be too soon..."

"I can't wait any longer."

"Just...try to be gentle, okay?" she asked.

It had been a long time since they'd had anal sex. At least while Gloria had still been pregnant, he'd been more careful with her when they'd fucked.

"I won't hurt you," he repeated, grabbing onto her hip after he'd finished stretching her asshole open.

Gloria felt her husband line his cock up against her asshole. She could feel his hard tip against her slightly stretched sphincter.

"I'm going to push inside you," he said, grabbing her hair in one hand, and taking his cock in the other.

"Yes, Henry."

Gloria winced, then whimpered as he entered her.

"Are you okay, babygirl?"

"Just go slowly."

He seemed to be having a hard time holding himself back...Gloria pressed back against him as she took another deep breath, opening her legs and arching her back.

"Oh," he moaned. "Good girl," he said. "Good girl, Gloria."

Gloria gripped her pillows hard, not wanting Henry to know how much he was hurting her.

She didn't want to anger him.

Gloria couldn't forget how he'd told her—when they'd first started dating—that he would leave her if she couldn't please him.

He bent her over and started thrusting harder and deeper inside her.

Gloria moaned...in pain, but she did her best to make it sound as though she were moaning in pleasure.

Somehow, she would make it work. Eventually she would be healed up and would be ready to have vaginal sex again...and she wasn't sure if that was a bad or a good thing.

Henry started moaning, and Gloria tensed. The pull inside her was painful. "More lube."

He squirted more lube on his cock before he dove deep inside her. Gloria grabbed onto the headboard, holding tightly. "Baby, not too loud. Don't wake Eva."

He groaned. "Gloria. Shut the fuck up."

She closed her eyes, willing it to be over soon...she was more concerned about waking the baby than she was about the pain she was in.

"Henry," she whispered.

He grabbed her around her neck, his other hand wrenching her hair. He went at her hard.

"I love you," she whispered again.

He pulled her back by her hair so that he could kiss her. "I love you, too, babygirl."

A month later, Gloria had an appointment scheduled for her daughter. While she was there, Henry asked the doctor—who was a pediatrician, not a gynecologist—to check Gloria out.

"The doctor doesn't have time for this,” Gloria argued.

"I can check you," the doctor said. "Are you having trouble with your stitches?"

"No," Gloria said, uncomfortable.

"We want a progress report on her recovery," Henry said.

Which was fairly creative, in Gloria's opinion. He hadn't explicitly said he wanted to know if she could have sex yet, but she knew what he was doing.

Awkwardly, Gloria got onto the table, handing Eva over to Henry.

"Looks like you're healing up nicely," the doctor said.

Gloria quickly got off the table and started putting her clothes back on. "Thank you."

"I'll leave you to get dressed. Stop by the reception desk to check out, and to schedule a three-month checkup for little Eva.”

As soon as she was alone with him, Gloria said, "That was incredibly embarrassing, Henry."

"But the good news is that we can have sex again," he said, giving her a look.

*She knew what he meant...that they wouldn't still be having painful anal sex—*at least not as often—*and they would be doing it more often.*

"I still need you to be gentle with me the first few times," Gloria said, snapping her bra into place and tugging her panties up her thighs.

"Of course," he said.

But when they got into bed together that night, Henry climbed on top of her, roughly pulling off her panties so that she was lying naked beneath him.

*Gloria had been insecure about her body **before** pregnancy...now with an extra ten pounds that she still hadn't lost from having Eva, along with the new stretch marks she had developed, she wasn't feeling sexy.*

Henry pinned her down as he began kissing her neck, his body pressing down against hers as he licked and sucked the sensitive skin of her neck and jawline.

Gloria attempted to cover her body, burrowing beneath the blankets and sheets surrounding them. She flinched when he pulled away the sheet she had strategically positioned over her thighs.

"What's the matter," he asked, his eyes drinking in her nude body hungrily.

"I look terrible."

"Shit Gloria, you look better than ever. Your tits are huge, and your curves are luscious."

He reached down to tweak her nipples. It felt good; her nipples were still sensitive from her pregnancy and from having an infant.

"I hate my body," she said.

"Stop it," he said, taking her ample breasts in either hand, grinding his pelvis against hers. "You are perfect."

"Can we turn the lights out?" she asked.

"I want to see the look on your face when I'm finally inside your pussy again, babygirl."

"Remember to be gentle," she whispered, opening her legs for him.

"I'm not pushing inside you just yet," he said, still fondling her breasts and kissing, sucking, and licking her neck. "I haven't forgotten how to please you."

She moaned softly, willing herself to relax. He was making her feel good, he was turning her on...it had been so long since her husband had actually made love to her.

"That's it, baby. Let me make you feel good."

She moaned louder, and he pressed his mouth down on hers, kissing her long and hard as his hands moved down her nude body.

"God, I've missed your pussy," he said.

"I love you," she whispered.

He moved her thighs apart. "You're wet for me."

He lifted her thighs high above her head. She gasped when she felt his tongue against her.

"Henry," she whispered.

"Your cunt tastes better than ever," he said, his tongue slipping between the slick folds of her pussy.

She highly doubted that, but she ***could*** *still appreciate the fact that he was doing everything in his power to make her feel more confident.*

She was nervous about him seeing her body, and about it hurting when they finally had sex. She'd been so scared that Henry was hurting their baby that she had asked him not to fuck her again until after Eva was born.

He lapped deep between her folds, then he slowly licked inside her, spreading her lips wide open, tasting her juices as he worked his way up to her clit.

She moaned loudly as he took her clit between his lips, rubbing the top with the end of his strong, wet tongue as he gently sucked with his lips and mouth.

He pinned her down firmly onto the mattress, not allowing her to squirm or to resist the intensity of what he was doing to her; he simply ravished her.

She panted, trying her hardest to keep her screams controlled as her husband caused the most exquisite, erotic feelings of pleasure to consume her entire body.

"Let it out, baby."

She didn't want to wake Eva, though... and honestly, most especially, she didn't want that amazing erotic moment to be interrupted or spoiled in any way.

He reached up to grab her right boob, twisting her nipple and being rewarded by the fresh gush of wetness Gloria produced, leaking onto his dick as he fucked her, as turned on as she was.

Deeming her drenched pussy wet enough, Henry carefully placed his body over hers. Gloria spread her legs wide as she felt Henry line his cock up with her opening.

"Henry, please be gentle," she said biting her lip as she looked up into the eyes of her husband.

"Of course, babygirl."

Seconds later, he was easing his cock inside her slippery, wet cunt. Gloria cringed as he stretched her, but she didn't ask him to stop.

Henry gave her a few seconds to get used to the feeling of him being inside her again.

Then he pushed all the way in, through her tightly sheathed vaginal opening, like a virgin again after she'd been stitched back together after having had Eva.

"Oh," she whimpered.

"Are you okay?" Henry asked.

"That was a lot. Don't move. Please, I need a moment to adjust," Gloria said.

Gloria was overwhelmed by the intensity of her feelings as Henry's cock impaled her...and the initial sting began to subside. She moaned in renewed pleasure as her husband twisted his hips, gliding his thick cock all against the inside of her pussy.

*"Fuck, it feels good, baby," she whimpered, wrapping her legs around his waist as she tightly wound her arms around her lover, holding him close to her, wanting him to keep doing **exactly** what he was doing in that moment, never wanting it to end.*

"You feel amazing," he said.

"I love you," she replied, running her fingers through his hair as she pulled his face down to hers.

Henry gave his wife a long, sensual kiss, then he moved his mouth down her neck, taking her breasts in his hands as he slowly, deeply began fucking her.

She whimpered at the feeling...she'd been cleared for sex, but it still didn't feel how it used to, like there was a tighter pull at the sensitive and delicate skin in her intimate areas.

Perhaps letting him assfuck her into oblivion for those weeks before he'd gotten back inside her cunt had something to do with it...it wasn't necessarily painful.

And if Gloria ignored the feel of the slight pull, sex truly felt incredible. It was the best they'd had in ages, without her pregnancy belly or her insecurities about her body to get in the way.

*"Oh god, Henry," she moaned, "keep doing that. Ugh, **yes,** baby!"*

*Encouraged by her overt horniness and eagerness to be fucked, Henry began thrusting deeper and harder, while still being somewhat gentle, and very tender with her...it was as though Henry knew **exactly** what she needed, and he was all too willing to deliver that to her.*

"Babygirl, open those gorgeous legs of yours a bit more...that's it. Good girl." He carefully positioned himself to fuck her deeper, slightly lifting her legs to make her already tight pussy feel even tighter.

*"Oh, god. Fucking **shit**, Henry!"*

"I'm glad you like that, baby," he said, kissing her lips before licking his index finger...then reaching between their bodies and beginning to rub slow, sensual circles over her clit.

The thing that truly made Gloria happiest was that her husband was being gentle and considerate as he was to her, as he slowly, gently brought her to orgasm.

Gloria shuddered and writhed in absolute joy and pleasure as she came, Henry's cock twitching deep inside her.

She moaned, burying her face against his shoulder as he gently lay on top of her.

"I love you, baby. And I love you for giving me our beautiful baby girl."

She sighed happily. Everything in her life was absolutely perfect: she had just made love to the love of her life, who also happened to be her husband, as their new beautiful, perfect baby daughter slept in their gorgeous modern penthouse in London, paid for by Gloria's dream career.

She couldn't imagine it ever getting any better than that.

And Gloria hadn't been wrong.

Ten months later, Gloria was back in the delivery room... that time, to give birth to her twin girls.

She delivered them vaginally, having already consulted with the cosmetic surgeon about having stretch mark removal and vaginal rejuvenation... the twins had ravaged her body just as they had her heart, but her body was far worse for the wear, while her heart was more tender than ever before.

Gloria loved being a mother.

But she despised being pregnant.

She hated being bloated, constipated, nauseous, and irritable... and typically was all the above when she was in her best health.

Pregnancy cruelly emphasized all her chronic ailments, along with her complete exhaustion from working on a new novel...the same one she had been writing since she and Henry had gotten pregnant with Eva. Pregnancy and motherhood certainly weren't synonymous with getting a novel written, as Gloria had discovered that early on. She tried to work out and to work on her novel while Eva slept in her swing or her carrier, but only a quarter of the time was she able to get anything done, no matter how she tried to multitask.

She barely had time to brush her teeth or shower, let alone to poop.

Of course, when Eva had been tiny—and especially after Gloria had gotten pregnant with the twins—Henry had been incredibly helpful.

It wasn't a long labor. Gloria delivered without any complications, and she'd carried the twins what was considered full term for a duo pregnancy.

The delivery had been incredibly painful, however. She had a lot more tearing with the twins than she had with Eva, but the joy of seeing her two perfect babies made her pain sting less intensely. She held the newborns against her chest before the nurses took them to be weighed and to see if they would need to go to the NICU.

Henry stood beside her head, stroking her hair as he stared down at her and their babies.

"I love you so much, Gloria," he said, kissing her forehead.

"I love you too," she whispered, holding her babies and feeling more love in that moment than ever before in her life.

Gloria's mother had come to England for the delivery, too, and Gloria had been grateful to have her mother there with her, just in case Henry hadn't given her what she needed, which was sometimes the case; not so much since she'd been having his babies for him, however.

"What are their names?" the nurse asked, coming to take the first twin from Gloria's arms.

Henry waited for the baby to be placed in his arms as Gloria replied, "Jemima Joanne is the first one, and Shoshannah Cheyenne is baby number two."

They'd decided that, as with Eva, they would give the twins each a nickname...Jem for Jemima, and Cheye for Shoshannah Cheyenne.

"Those are beautiful names," the nurse said, smiling at Gloria.

Gloria smiled back at her, then she looked down at Cheye in her arms. It was physically painful for her to let go of her babies, although she knew that as soon as they sent the babies home with her and Henry, she would long for a few moments of peace and for being on her own.

She finally gave Cheye to her husband, then she sighed, feeling empty...for the first time in over eight months, she didn't have her twins with her. For the first time since their conception, they weren't inside her body or in her arms, and it was an alien feeling for her.

"Are you okay?" Henry asked, stroking her sweaty hair out of her face.

"I miss them," Gloria whispered.

"Oh, it's okay, baby," Henry said. "Just enjoy the peace and quiet while you can, okay?"

She nodded, feeling tears come to her eyes.

Henry knelt beside her. "Baby, it's okay."

"I know," she whispered, feeling ridiculous for being so emotional.

He gently kissed her, then held her close to him as he carefully hugged her. "I love you, Gloria."

"I love you, too."

She tried to smile at him, but she was truly aching.

"Do you want me to have your mother bring Eva in here?" he asked, figuring that having her daughter nearby would make her feel better.

"Henry?"

"Yes, darling?" he asked, sweetly running his fingers through her long, wet blond curls.

"It's always going to be good, like this. Right?" she asked, looking worriedly up into her husband's eyes.

He continued stroking her hair. "What do you mean?"

"You're madly in love with me right now. I just gave you twins."

"I ***do*** *love you, babygirl."*

"Henry, I know...I guess what I'm trying to say is...are you still going to be this loving toward me now that I'm not pregnant?"

He frowned. "Do you think I was only being 'kind' to you because you were pregnant?"

Feeling stupid, Gloria shrugged.

"I made a vow to take care of you, Gloria. I'm always going to take care of you."

She smiled as he leaned in and softly kissed her, praying he would always feel that way.

Two days later, Gloria was nearly asleep in her bed, Henry's warm body beside her, Eva in her crib beside Henry's side of the bed, and Jem and Cheye in their cribs beside Gloria's side of the bed...she insisted on the babies sleeping in the same room as them, being so afraid of SIDS and other terrible things that could happen to babies, and Henry had agreed, because otherwise he knew that Gloria wouldn't have slept at all.

Gloria figured that soon enough, she was going to have to put Eva in the nursery, as having all five of them sleeping in the same room wasn't going to work. With the twins waking and crying in the middle of the night, Gloria knew that Eva would be better off in the nursery, anyway. That way she and Henry wouldn't have three babies to cope with in the middle of the night.

Gloria reached over and began stroking her husband's back. He groaned softly, reaching back to twist his fingers through hers.

Seconds later, he rolled over to look at her, taking her face in his hands before kissing her softly. "I love you, baby."

"I love you, too," she moaned, kissing him back. "I'm so happy, Henry. You've given me everything I ever wanted."

"You've done the same for me, babygirl," he said, kissing her long and hard, then moaning, "Ugh. I wish we could fuck."

Gloria giggled. "That's not going to happen for quite some time, baby. I'm sorry." She frowned. "God, I'm in a lot of pain."

Henry nodded, stroking her face. "I know. I saw...I can't even imagine how badly that must hurt."

"I mean, of course they are worth it, but ***god****, it hurts."*

Gloria hadn't had time to think about how much pain she was in, or to even process all that had happened...her vaginal rip, the way her pelvic floor felt as though it were gaping open...she was utterly exhausted from the fast, fierce delivery...although she was incredibly grateful that both her deliveries had been quick and uncomplicated.

She started crying as it all pressed down on her. Her tears alarmed Henry.

"Are you in that much pain, babygirl?" he asked, drawing her close.

She buried her face against his chest, resting in his safe, strong embrace.

"Gloria?" Henry asked.

"I can't go through that again," she sobbed. "I love our babies, and I ***love*** *being a mother. I'd like to have more...my body just can't take it."*

"We'll talk later about it, sweetheart," he said, kissing her forehead.

Gloria had the feeling Henry wasn't going to make it easy for her to get out of not having more babies for him. She wanted to believe that she was more to him than a breeding factory, and that he'd love her just as much if they stopped at three; after all, three children was how many Vic had given him, and at least Gloria had given him as much as his ex-wife had.

She didn't want to admit that there was a possibility he loved her only when she was pregnant, when he could impregnate her, or while she was caring for an infant.

But, considering she'd found she was pregnant soon after they'd gotten back together, she'd never faced that reality before.

And she was terrified to do so.

Gloria found Henry just where she'd suspected that she would...lying on the sofa, wrapped in one of her throw blankets, resting his head on a pillow he must have snatched off the bed in the middle of the night, although Gloria wasn't sure how he'd managed to do so without waking her, as she was all but attuned to always be aware of her husband's presence...especially after not getting to be in it nearly as often as she wished to be.

She stood over the massive, heavily stuffed custom-made sofa... It was of buttery leather and was a cream color—probably not the color wisest to have in a home where there were three tiny children, but Gloria had been highly emotional and had been pregnant when she had ordered it, so she chose it in an altered mental and emotional state—and it was absolutely gorgeous, but she wished that her husband wasn't asleep on it most nights, for a number of reasons.

The main reason, however, was because she wanted him in bed beside her each night, as he should have been.

She knelt beside Henry, running her fingers through his hair, waking him. "Baby?"

Henry moaned loudly, stretching, then rolled over onto his back, looking at Gloria sheepishly. "Good morning, babygirl."

She smiled, leaning forward to kiss his forehead. "I love you."

He sighed. "I thought I'd be in trouble. I didn't realize I would be awakened with a gentle kiss after I didn't come home last night."

She smiled. "I certainly don't want to make you less eager to come home to me."

His face clouded. "Gloria, please."

"I'm not arguing. Scoot over."

He stared as she climbed underneath the blanket with him, curling her body against his, wrapping her arms around him as she cuddled into his chest.

He stroked her hair back, then he kissed her forehead. "I'm sorry about last night."

He always was.

"I don't want to talk about it," she said. "I just want you to cuddle with me."

"Of course," he said, kissing her lips softly... she could still smell the alcohol on his breath.

"I miss sleeping in bed with you."

"I'm here every night," she said.

"Do you know what else I miss?" he asked, holding her close.

Gloria mumbled against his chest, but she felt Henry's hands began to work over her body, down her back, as he used one of his legs to nudge her thighs apart.

She should have known...Henry was always so eager to fuck her, but not always willing to give her a kind, loving touch...

She allowed him to initiate sex, though. His left hand worked its way into her panties, his right hand easing inside her negligee top as his finger found her clit, teasing it gently as the fingers of his other hand slipped between her folds.

"Henry, I'm still tired," she said, moaning a bit in protest as he continued to try fucking her.

"Baby, we never get to do this anymore. Please," he said, working his mouth against her neck, knowing neck kisses were her weakness.

"If you'd sleep in our bed, it would be a lot easier," she mumbled, knowing she was going to let him fuck her.

She opened her legs to grant him better access. Gloria threw her head back and sighed as Henry's fingers worked their magic between her legs, teasing her folds and slowly working their way up her clit. He applied just the right amount of pressure, making her moan softly. "Henry."

"Just let go, babygirl," he said, circling her slowly, in deep strokes, imitating what he would be doing with his cock in a few moments.

His fingers slipped inside her, stretching her cunt open for him, feeling how wet she was. He looked down at her, smiling darkly.

"Maybe you are tired, babygirl, but you can't deny your body wants me."

"I do want you," she said, placing her hands on his face as she looked into his eyes.

"Kiss me," he said, and she leaned up to press her lips against his, moaning desperately into his mouth as his fingers worked their way deeper inside her, as he began applying a tantalizing pressure to her g-spot.

"Good girl," he said, kissing her neck as he reached up, pressing the fingers he'd just had inside her pussy against her mouth. Gloria took his fingers in her mouth, sucking her juices off him.

"You're going to clean my cock after I'm done fucking you, too, aren't you?" he asked.

"Yes, Henry," she replied.

Gloria had never been able to explain how or why he managed to make her go from zero to one hundred simply by talking to her, or by touching her, but every molecule of her body was set to melt in his presence.

"I'm going to fuck you hard, babygirl," he said, his voice deep and dark as he took his cock in one hand, guiding it against the opening of her pussy.

She looked at him as he focused on entering her. Gloria whimpered, gasping as his cock stretched her.

"You're still so fucking tight," he said, as he sheathed himself entirely inside her.

Gloria moaned in response, and Henry brought his hand up to her mouth, making her suck his fingers to muffle the sounds of her whimpers.

She'd spent so long muffling the sounds of her pleasure—since the babies slept in her and Henry's bedroom—she couldn't remember the last time she and Henry had filthy, wild sex...no wonder he was starting to get antsy.

Her husband had needs. He needed that BDSM aspect of their relationship...something that he'd been unable to indulge in since they'd gotten back together.

Gloria hadn't been back with him for a month, after all, before she'd discovered that she was pregnant with his baby, and they had both agreed that sex as rough as they'd typically had it was too much for her while pregnant...and since she'd barely been healed from the first baby when she'd gotten pregnant with the twins, it had been ages since Henry had really been able to let go and indulge in her. She knew she needed to be more open minded and patient with him.

"Baby," she said, rolling onto her side, wrapping her legs around him as she pulled him deeper inside her.

"I love you, Gloria," he said, beginning to thrust.

She whimpered...god, it felt amazing to have him inside her that way. He *was* an amazing lover, although sometimes he was too rough with her...sometimes he genuinely hurt her, but somehow Gloria managed to forget about those times, when she was missing him so desperately, and when she wanted him to fuck her so badly...

And when he told her that he loved her...well, those words had gotten her to do absolutely anything for him.

He started fucking her progressively harder. Gloria started to moan and whimper as he spread her legs further apart so that he could fuck her deeper...it felt amazing, as he was hitting parts of her body that hadn't been touched in ages.

"God, baby," she whimpered.

"Arch your back, babygirl. I'm going harder," he warned, grabbing her behind her back and lifting her body so that he was fucking into her like she was a fleshlight.

He was fucking her hard and nasty, and Gloria was loving every second of it.

Henry began grinding his dick deep inside her, twisting his hips to brush against her walls, making her tremble

"God," she moaned.

"Not yet. Don't come yet, babygirl."

"I... I need to," she panted.

"Not yet."

Henry lowered his voice, moaning, whispering into her ear, "I need to feel your cunt clenching around my cock as I squirt my cum inside your fertile pussy."

Gloria about lost it, moaning loudly and biting down on her lip as she looked into his eyes, feeling as though she would combust.

Henry moaned, loud and low, and he buried himself deep inside her, then said, "Cum for me, baby."

Gloria immediately relaxed, letting herself go, as the tingles rose from her feet, her lower back, exploding inside her pussy as she clenched down hard on Henry's ejaculating cock.

Her whole body shook from the pleasure he was giving her. He kept twisting deep inside her, his cock grinding hard against her g spot, prolonging that exquisite feeling ravishing every molecule of her being.

She moaned, almost screaming as Henry covered her mouth with his, muffling her cries of pleasure.

He held her firmly as they both kept cumming, as Henry's cock unloaded more spunk inside her channel. She nearly passed out, cumming so hard and long, remaining in that intense orgasmic state.

Finally, he settled his body over hers, kissing her lips gently. She sighed, exhausted.

"God, babygirl, that was incredible," Henry murmured against her neck, his breath hot on her skin.

Gloria could only groan in response. She could still feel Henry buried almost painfully deep inside her already sore pussy, pulsing as she twitched around him.

He kissed her mouth again, then gently began easing out from where he had impaled her.

"Are you okay, baby?" he asked, his voice soft.

She nodded. "Just... already exhausted." She smiled, then reached up, playing with his hair.

"I love you, Gloria," he said, pulling her close, his softened dick soaking wet, resting against her thigh.

"I love you."

He kissed her forehead. "Why don't you go take a shower while I cook breakfast?"

"Really?"

"Yes, baby." He smiled at her like she was the center of his universe, and Gloria felt tears come to her eyes as she smiled back at him.

He stood, pulling his clothes back into place as Gloria lay still on the sofa, naked and tangled in the blankets, with her bra discarded and her panties around one ankle.

He smiled. "I wore you out, didn't I?"

She nodded, and he reached down, taking her hands in his, helping her up.

She flinched at the pain between her legs.

"Did I hurt you?"

"It was worth it," Gloria sighed, pulling her panties up and tying her robe around her waist.

"I don't want to hurt you," he said. "I was too rough."

"Henry...I know you missed it."

He met her eyes, and she knew that he was aware exactly what she was talking about.

"I do. But... Gloria, you're my wife."

She nodded. "Yes?"

"The mother of my children."

She swallowed. "Henry..."

"Babygirl."

"You're...you're not..."

"Not what?" he asked, staring at her unblinkingly.

"Getting your fix somewhere else?" she asked, her voice trembling as she spoke.

"Are you fucking joking, Gloria?" he demanded.

She wished more than anything that she could take those words back.

"I make love to you, and you ask me if I'm being unfaithful?"

"I only meant—"

"You know what? Make your own damn breakfast, Gloria. I'm going back to bed."

"Baby, please—"

"I'm not discussing this with you now," he said, heading toward their bedroom.

"Henry."

She was crying openly, but she was afraid to approach him...he was *so* angry with her.

It was all her fault, spoiling a beautiful, loving moment with her Henry, the love of her life...they were both under a lot of stress, but she still should have been more considerate of him.

She let him go, Henry slamming the heavy sliding wooden door shut and clicking the lock into place.

Gloria had tears streaming down her face, and her heart was breaking...it was a huge mindfuck, going from being so happy, in love, having Henry back at last, to being hurt by his actions, being upset she'd hurt *him*.

She wanted to go after him, to apologize, to explain to him why she had asked that question...

Gloria was aching...although they hadn't partaken in BDSM play when they'd had sex just then, she still felt she needed that comfort and connection from him, to be held, kissed, and cuddled...it was what every woman wanted after being made love to, but for Henry to shut her out as he had...it made her heart ache.

She *did* desperately need a shower, as his cum was leaking slowly down her pussy, puddling in her panties, and she felt gross and very sore; Gloria would have loved to soak in the tub, even, but she knew her babies would awaken soon, and she needed to make sure that they had their breakfasts and got their diapers changed.

Their needs took precedence over hers, of course...as well as Henry's.

But Gloria didn't mind, as long as he was being sweet to her...although the honeymoon had ended quite some time ago.

Gloria was also terrified that the only reason Henry had been so sweet to her for so long was due to her being pregnant, or having just given birth...

But she knew Henry, and she knew his voracious appetite for rough, kinky sex.

The way he'd looked at her...god help her, but it had seemed as if he were trying to tell her that one of her biggest fears had been realized.

That Henry had been getting his kinky fix somewhere other than in their bed, and in her arms.

2

CHAPTER TWO

"Mummy!"

Gloria placed Eva's carefully sliced toast in front of her, with just a touch of butter, perfectly golden brown. She'd tried everything to get Eva to eat breakfast, because the sweet baby preferred to goof off all throughout the meal—as Gloria tried to feed the twins—then once she'd finally gotten them fed and everyone cleaned up, Eva would announce that she was hungry...and the chaos commenced, never ending until bedtime, and sometimes even later than that.

It was no wonder that Gloria hadn't been able to get much of her new novel written since she'd gotten pregnant the first time...second time, truthfully, as Eva was her rainbow baby. When Gloria had first moved to England (Blackpool at the time) with Henry—before they'd gotten married—she'd gotten pregnant with him, but they'd lost the baby.

Gloria had been devastated, and she'd only been hurt worse when Henry had become distant. It had seemed to Gloria as though Henry had blamed her for miscarrying. This had caused a rift between them, when Gloria had been completely isolated from every other living being, ostracized from her family, not only for moving to be with Henry, but also for publishing her erotica novel, which had made her none too popular with her right-wing political family. Her father was a former state senator for Georgia, after all. Gloria had an image to uphold for his sake.

Even as Gloria was feeding the twins their tiny pieces of pureed fruit, she was racking her brain to figure out how on earth she was going to make up with Henry... even though part of her still didn't think it was her fault. She had truly believed he had been trying to tell her he was having an affair.

She was so glad that he *wasn't*, but she was heartbroken he had shut her out. She wanted the kind, loving, even *gentle* version of Henry she'd had that morning, waking him lovingly before making love on the sofa...

But she could fall apart later. For now, she had two infants and a toddler to care for, and that alone was more than she could manage.

As much as Gloria deeply and desperately loved her daughters, she sometimes longed to stay in bed, to sleep in, to indulge in a self-care day, to get her nails done, or to even spend an afternoon uninterrupted, glued to her laptop, writing a new novel...

There were days Gloria was terrified she would never write another book.

During breakfast, Cheye pooped in her fresh diaper, and Gloria had to scoop her and Jem up, making Eva leave her plate of toast—that she was finally willing to eat—as she took the twins to the nursery, setting Jem inside her crib as she put stacking rings in front of Eva, taking Cheye and placing her on a blanket to change her massively disastrous poop diaper.

As she was finishing changing Cheye's diaper, Jem pooped her diaper, and the twins both started giggling in tandem, almost as though they planned it.

If the sound of her babies' laughter hadn't been Gloria's favorite sound, she might have burst into tears of sheer exhaustion, as the poop erupted from Jem's diaper and Gloria's own dirty lace panties started rubbing her raw.

She tried not to think about how Henry was asleep in bed as she did all the parenting and caretaking on her own. Maybe it's what she deserved suspecting Henry was sleeping around on her.

Finally, Gloria had the twins cleaned up. She had one on either hip as she washed her hands, then made Eva—much to her eldest daughter's displeasure—wash her hands, too, because she needed to finish feeding them breakfast.

As soon as she got back to the kitchen, Eva bypassed her plate of toast and went to the pantry, asking for a biscuit.

Gloria placed the twins in their highchairs. "Eat your toast, baby, I'll get you a biscuit when you finish."

Eva turned and looked up and at Gloria with her big brown eyes, so much like her father's. "Please, Mummy!"

"Just a moment, darling," Gloria said, as she went back to feeding the twins.

"Mummy," Eva cried, pitifully.

Gloria sighed. "Come sit in your chair and finish your toast, or no biscuit, Eva."

Still hiccuping sobs, Eva came and sat in her chair. Gloria smoothed back Eva's reddish hair—she wasn't sure why her first born was a redhead, save the Henry's other children were redheads—soothingly, cursing Henry for not being there, so that Eva wouldn't be upset. Henry thought Gloria was too soft on Eva and that she spoiled her, but Gloria had always known she'd be the kind of mother who spoiled her children.

As soon as Eva took one bite of her toast, however, she was happy again, smiling her cute, toothy little smile up at Gloria, making her heart melt.

The twins were happy to gum their fruit and get it all over themselves. At least their diapers were clean, she supposed.

Soon Eva's toast was gone. She waited patiently as Gloria finished feeding her sisters, and as she cleaned them up.

She picked up the twins and grabbed Eva a biscuit, which made the twins want one as well.

Gloria's own breakfast ended up being half a biscuit that she split with the twins.

She had the twins burped and in their swings as Eva watched *Bluey* on TV, and, exhausted, Gloria collapsed onto the same sofa that her husband had fucked her senseless on, only a few hours before.

Gloria knew already that it was going to be a very long day.

She had just fed her children their lunch when Henry finally surfaced from the bedroom. He was all smiles for the babies, scooping Eva up and playing with her, then kissing the twins on top of their fuzzy blond heads.

He didn't acknowledge Gloria, who took the opportunity of him watching the children to clean the disaster of the kitchen, not having had the opportunity to clean up after breakfast, then going right in to fixing lunch...the juicer needed washing, as did the blender; she'd made Eva a grilled cheese for lunch, so the skillet was in the sink, and the chopping board was caked with dried fruit.

The countertops were sticky, as was the table, as were the twins. She grabbed a warm cloth and gently wiped down the twins' faces as Henry pointedly ignored her.

"If you can watch them for a bit, I've got some cleaning to do," Gloria said, too afraid to meet Henry's eyes, as it had taken all the courage she possessed simply to speak to him, with the mood he was in.

"Do what you must, Gloria," he said coldly.

She quickly finished cleaning her children's faces and hands, then turned away and hurried back into the kitchen before Henry could see the tears filling her eyes, which were dripping down her face by the time she tossed the wet cloth onto the counter.

She buried her face in her hands, willing herself to stop crying. She had only a small window of time to get the kitchen cleaned and some laundry done.

In about fifteen minutes, she had the kitchen clean, dishes washed, and the dishwasher running, before she crossed the kitchen to the open-concept laundry room, which was beside the pantry, with marble floors as the rest of the penthouse had.

Perhaps marble was an unforgiving material for flooring in the home of a family with three babies, but Gloria had many plush rugs that she spread out across the floors—especially the stairs—once Eva had begun to learn to walk.

She nearly fainted in fear as she added laundry powder to the load she was starting, thinking about what her life was going to be like very soon, when her just-turned-one twins began running around like their older sister. She truly was never going to have a moment's rest ever again, much less a stolen moment to get her novel written. So exhausted she wanted to cry, Gloria considered how complicated her life had become...and how desperately she needed her husband's help.

She needed to talk to Henry, but after that morning, she was afraid to.

Once she had a load in the washer, she went back to the living room, where the twins were getting sleepy and Eva was getting bratty.

"Please, Daddy!"

Gloria bent down and picked Eva up. "What's she wanting?"

"A biscuit," Henry said, rolling his eyes. "I told her she just ate lunch."

"You had a biscuit this morning, darling," Gloria said, smoothing back her baby's hair.

"I ate all my lunch. Please, Mummy," she said, pouting in a way Gloria could never say 'no' to.

"Oh, sweetheart, you can't have a biscuit after every meal," Gloria said, kissing her daughter's head.

"Why not, Mummy?"

Gloria sighed. "It will hurt your tummy, and you won't be hungry to eat your dinner when you wake from your nap later."

"No, Mummy, my tummy doesn't hurt, and I promise I'll be hungry!"

"Not now, baby. If you eat all your dinner, I'll let you have a biscuit then, okay?"

Eva sighed dramatically, resting her head against her mother's chest. "Okay."

Henry was frowning at Gloria, when she dared to meet his eyes. "I told you you're spoiling her."

Gloria felt a couple of tears slip down her cheeks. "I'm doing my best," she whispered.

Henry shook his head, and Eva asked, "Are you sad, Mummy?"

"No, Mummy is fine, baby," Gloria said, smiling at her. "Are you ready for your nap?"

"Read to me?"

"Of course I will, darling," Gloria said, kissing Eva.

She looked at Henry. "Would you like to help me put them down for their naps?"

He was holding both twins, who were already asleep. He followed her into the nursery, where Gloria had finally been convinced to allow the children to sleep, once the twins had turned a year old.

It had been a battle to get Eva on board. She'd gotten to where she insisted upon sleeping in bed between her mother and father, which Gloria had been entirely okay with, but Henry, of course, wanted to get the babies out of their bedroom as soon as possible. Gloria understood that, as Henry wanted to have access to his wife, and he certainly wanted to have sex more often...and more adventurous sex, which he hadn't had for a long time.

She halted that train of thought almost immediately, as she didn't want to think about what had happened that morning, the thing that had caused that rift between her and Henry, after such a beautiful, intimate moment together.

Confronting Henry again—especially when he was already in a terrible mood—was a terrible idea, no matter how desperately the two of them needed to discuss their issues.

Gloria settled Eva in her bed, stroking her hair. "What book would you like me to read?"

"The one you wrote me," Eva said.

Gloria smiled, walking over to the bookshelf against the far wall of Eva's bedroom, selecting the one—and only—children's book that Gloria had ever published...and she'd chosen to publish it under a pen name, rather than under her given name, Gloria Alexander, which was the name under which she published her romantic/erotica books, and how she'd made her *own* fortune, shamelessly going against the family fortune and her political heiress status, soiling the "good" southern Alexander name by shamefully publishing her smut.

Truthfully, in the 1800s, the Alexanders had fought with the Confederation and had owned slaves...not to mention the sexual scandals on her father's side of the family.

The Alexanders had been into politics for generations, and it certainly showed...yet she was still the black sheep of the family, bringing shame and scandal upon them all through her writing career.

Hypocrisy at its finest, but there was a reason that the only "family" Gloria considered herself to have was her mother...and her best friend, Cynthia, whom she'd lived with in Los Angeles, and who was Eva, Cheye, and Jem's godmother.

Gloria selected Eva's favorite book, one about her favorite animal—a dog—getting lost from her mother and siblings before she found her way home, from the help of a little gurl who had come across the pup in the park, reuniting the puppy with her family.

Gloria didn't enjoy writing children's books, but she would have done anything in the universe for her own children.

Eva insisted upon Gloria reading the book twice, and by the last third of the book the second time through, Eva was asleep.

Gloria gently kissed her forehead, then turned down the lights and left her sleeping in her bed, cozy and safe, and being watched by the baby monitor, of course...Henry had asked when Gloria was going to stop using the baby monitor with Eva, but she wasn't ready to do so yet...maybe by the time Eva was old enough to start school.

Gloria knew that it would be in her children's best interests if she sent them to preschool at least a couple of days a week, so that when they began school at school-age, it wouldn't be such a shock to their systems, and they'd know better how to socialize with other children in an environment not controlled by her, and with her not being in their presence, but at the same time, it killed her to think about being away from her daughters for any amount of time.

It was a reality that Gloria was going to soon face, however, as Eva had turned three recently.

For the moment, though, as Gloria carefully and quietly closed the door behind her, leaving little Eva asleep, she knew that there was no better time than the present to try speaking to Henry about the argument they'd had that morning.

Henry was sitting on the sofa, flipping through channels until he found a football match. Gloria sat beside him, and he ignored her as he continued staring at the giant screen television.

She took a deep breath. "Henry, darling, can we talk about this morning?"

"What's there to talk about? You accused me of cheating, *after* I made love to you." He turned to look at her. "How do you think that made me feel, Gloria?"

She felt those damned tears she'd been fighting all morning and early afternoon spring to her eyes again. "I'm so sorry. I never should have said that."

"But isn't it bad enough that, after all I have done for you, Gloria, how good I've been to you throughout the pregnancies, and how I've comforted you and taken care of you, that you could come to the conclusion I'm being unfaithful?"

"That's not what I meant!" she cried. "I thought you were trying to tell me that you'd been...well, curbing your appetite somehow."

"What makes you say that?"

She shrugged. "I know that you're not happy with a tame sex life."

"Gloria, we don't even *have* a sex life anymore."

She flinched. It was painful, him speaking those words to her...she'd done so much for him—those painful anal sessions, when she'd still been healing, not to mention giving birth to his children and allowing him to fuck her before she was comfortable with her recovery—and he was discounting all of *that,* saying that her efforts had been in vain, because they apparently may as well have not been fucking at all, according to Henry's logic.

"Don't look at me like that, Gloria," he said, frowning. "You know as well as I do that you stopped trying as soon as you knew that you had me locked down."

She clenched her jaw. "When was that, exactly?"

He looked directly into her eyes as he said, "When you gave birth to our daughter."

The tears couldn't be stopped, then. Gloria buried her face in her hands, turning away from Henry so that he wouldn't see her cry...although he knew exactly what she was doing.

The pain cut so deep Gloria had to curl into herself, trying to hold herself together.

Henry sighed, pausing the game. She felt the sofa shift as he got up from his seat and came to sit on the other side of her. She felt his hands touch her arms as he began to try to pry her into a sitting position.

"Gloria, look at me, please."

Gloria forced herself to do as Henry asked, tears streaming down her face. She was ashamed, being so emotional and easily hurt. She knew better. She'd known from the time she and Henry started dating that it wasn't going to be an easy ride, and he wasn't going to be gentle and cautious with her...still she had begun to expect him to be. She *was* his wife, after all...she couldn't help but think...shouldn't he have *wanted* to make her happy, rather than to make her cry, constantly being forced to fight her emotions?

She met his eyes, seeing a torturous expression there...he wasn't happy either, she realized.

That fact hurt her even worse.

"I don't want to see you crying. I'm trying to be honest, babygirl. I will always be honest with you."

"I know, Henry."

"Come here," he said, and she folded into his embrace. She took a deep breath, inhaling his scent, although he mostly still smelled like cigarette smoke and alcohol. He spent more time at that damned pub with his drinking buddies than he did at home with his wife and daughters.

He stroked her back. "I'm sorry I upset you."

"I'm so sorry about this morning, Henry. I never meant to hurt you."

"I would *never* be unfaithful to you, Gloria."

All she'd ever wanted was for this man to love her. Here he was, telling her just how much he did...but she still couldn't stop her tears. Those tears refused to stop before her negative emotions had fully been displayed and acknowledged.

"Are you okay, Gloria?" he asked. "You haven't calmed down at all."

"I think...I just need to get it all out," she said, hiccuping.

He stroked her back. "It's going to be okay. Babygirl, I'm not going anywhere."

"Good," she cried, wrapping her arms tightly around him and burying her face against his chest.

He kissed the top of her head. "It's going to be fine, babygirl."

After a few more moments of being held and allowed to cry, Gloria's sobs began to ease.

She was grateful to Henry for allowing her to cry it out...that was exactly what she'd needed...to be free to feel and to release her pent up, smothered emotions...and for her husband to comfort her.

"We still need to do something about this," he said, his breath warm against her face.

"We do. I think having this conversation has been a good start."

"I can think of a good finish. We still have time before they should wake from their nap," Henry said pointedly.

"What's that?"

He placed one finger underneath her chin, lifting her gaze to his face. "Inside you."

Gloria smiled. "I'd like a repeat of this morning...and maybe we can end it better."

"Loving on each other instead of fighting?"

"Exactly," Gloria said, sighing happily as Henry worked his mouth from her lips, down her neck, then back to her mouth, kissing her deeply, his tongue slipping inside.

She moaned softly, and he wrapped his hands around her waist...she loved the feel of his hands on her, so strong, dominating, and demanding.

Sometimes she *did* miss aspects of their BDSM lifestyle...but mostly, she was debating which would be worse: going through another pregnancy or going back to being Henry's submissive.

She hated having thoughts like that.

Henry scooped her up and carried her down the hallway into their bedroom, where he placed her gently on the bed before he went back to close and lock the bedroom door...now that Eva was walking everywhere there was always a possibility of her walking in on her mother and father fucking...that was something that she and Henry never wanted their children to have to experience.

He came over to her, beginning to undress as he stared down at her hungrily, in a way that turned Gloria on *so much.*

"You're beautiful, my darling," he said, stripping down to nothing.

She stared at his cock, licking her lips.

"Mmm, babygirl," he said, "you want to taste my cock?"

She nodded. "I need it."

He moaned. "Good. Take your clothes off."

She untied her robe and slipped off her top, her breasts springing free. She sighed as the cool air of the bedroom hit her skin, as Henry's hungry gaze intensified.

He climbed onto their bed, straddling her face, holding himself over her. His cock was hard, and he was eager for her to take him in her mouth.

Gloria started to take off her panties, but Henry said, "Not yet."

She shivered with sexual excitement and arousal. She stuck out her tongue, brushing it against his cock head, licking off his little bead of precum.

"God, girl," he said.

Gloria smiled, glad that she could still affect her husband so deeply, that she still turned him on.

She circled his cock with her tongue, sucking his tip between her lips, lapping around him.

"Fuck, Gloria," Henry moaned.

She smiled naughtily, knowing that she still had what it took to really get her husband off...that morning had been a fluke.

He still loved, needed, and wanted her, and one day, they would be able to reignite the BDSM aspect of their relationship...she was sure of it.

The only thing that Gloria was *not* certain of was whether being in a 24/7 submissive/dominant relationship was something that she wanted for her and Henry's marriage, but for that moment, she was thoroughly enjoying making her husband moan as his cock twitched inside her mouth.

She held his gaze as she sucked him in deeper, slowly easing her mouth down over the rest of his shaft, as his head brushed against the back of her throat. Gloria opened her throat, beginning to breathe through her nose so that she would be able to take Henry deep inside.

She could tell from the way he was grabbing onto her hair that he intended to fuck her face, hard. Their BDSM dynamic was already getting back into full swing...Gloria hoped she would be able to give Henry everything that he needed, that she hadn't lost her edge, and she hoped she could still do everything that he wanted her to do.

She prayed she was still able to please him...although she was quite certain that wasn't something that she should have been praying for.

Henry grabbed onto the back of her head. "Open wide, babygirl, I'm gonna fuck you hard."

She whimpered as he shoved his cock deep inside her throat, so that his balls were smashed hard against her lips. She knew if she were able to open her mouth a little bit wider, he would have tried to shove those inside, as well...he'd done the same to her ass, splitting her asshole when he'd been unable to fuck her pussy.

As he thrust deep inside her mouth, Gloria maintained eye-contact with him, trying her hardest not to show him how much she was struggling, but the tears streaming down her face at being choked so hard with his cock gave her away.

He seemed to enjoy her struggle, though, as he reached down to grab one breast in his hand, squeezing it as he grazed her nipple with his thumb, making her shudder.

"I know you like that, babygirl. I'm going to cum straight down your throat, coating your stomach with my hot load.

"Then I'm going to eat your sweet pussy until my cock is hard again, and I'm going to fuck you senseless...I'm aiming to put another baby inside you tonight, Gloria."

She gasped, then choked so hard that Henry ended up having to ease his cock out of her throat. "Are you okay?"

She nodded, taking him in her hand as she guided him back down her throat, swirling her tongue around his shaft as she sucked, constricting around him.

He slapped her tits as they bounced, as she fucked his cock hard with her face...she winced, and he loved that, grabbing both her breasts and squeezing, cupping, and rubbing them gently, to ease the sting of his slap.

He'd never slapped her tits before, and Gloria wasn't sure she liked it, but since she was currently choking on his cock, she couldn't have protested, even if she'd wanted to.

She kept sucking, loving the feel of Henry massaging her sensitive breasts...his harsh treatment had heightened her sensitivity, making her appreciate his sexual prowess even more.

He *always* knew what he was doing; it was one of the reasons she had fallen in love with Henry, after all...he had been her sexual awakening, the first man who had ever made her feel anything at all, and she had fallen in love because of it; he had taught her that she was a submissive.

Sometimes, though, Gloria wondered if she really *was* a submissive. Henry had made her his, and she hadn't had much choice in the matter...she'd looked for his replacement in every other man she'd been with.

The only three men she'd been with who hadn't been dominants were Javier (the man she'd loved the most, other than her husband, of course), her ex-husband, Bryson, who had broken her, and Noel...a true idiot, but if not for him, she never would have reunited with Henry.

Gloria supposed she truly was a submissive, then.

She moaned, looking into Henry's eyes as he really went at her, as she gagged and as tears poured down her cheeks. She had nearly reached her limit, had been deprived of the ability to take a deep breath for too long, when Henry grunted loudly, and she felt his hot cum pour down her throat.

She held his gaze, moaning as she gently swallowed.

He groaned, easing his cock out of her throat. She carefully cleaned him off with her mouth and tongue.

He knelt between her legs, wrapping his arms around her and pulling her close as he kissed her, long and hard on her mouth, tasting himself on her.

"I love you," she whispered.

“I love you, babygirl,” he said, pulling her onto him so that he was underneath her.

She wrapped her legs around him. “That was amazing.”

He laughed, taking her face in his hands. “Isn’t that my line, babygirl?”

She shrugged. “I enjoyed myself.”

“I enjoyed you thoroughly.” He grabbed her ass, squeezing hard, then he reached forward and shoved the lace between her legs aside, touching her swollen labia, making her moan.

“We’re just getting started, baby,” he said. “By the way, what were you thinking about, right before I came?”

She felt her brow furrow. “What?”

“You were somewhere else.”

Before she knew what had happened, he had her underneath him, on her stomach...she had no idea how he’d managed to do it, but he was able to do a lot of things that surprised Gloria.

“You weren’t thinking about me,” he said.

“I was! I was thinking about how much I love you—*fuck!*”

She flinched and jumped as he brought his hand down, hard, on her ass. He quickly gave her two more hard slaps, stinging.

“Henry, what the hell?”

“What were you thinking about, Gloria?” he asked, waiting.

“I *told* you, baby, I was—goddamn!”

He slapped her ass three more times...her skin was stinging, and she knew she couldn’t take much more...she wasn’t going to be able to sit comfortably for days, as it was.

Henry showed no signs of stopping...apparently, Gloria had done something wrong, yet again...some unwritten rule of BDSM according to Henry, and thus she had hell to pay for it.

“Tell me. I can slap your ass all night, Gloria, but how long can your flesh take the blows?”

“I was thinking about how much I *love you*!” she cried out, sobbing into her pillow.

“Bullshit.” He flipped her over. She winced as her sore ass hit the sheets, the lace of her panties feeling like sandpaper against her painful flesh, but she looked up into her husband’s eyes as she said, “I told you, baby. I was thinking about how much I love you.”

He frowned, then without warning, he pried her thighs apart, opening her legs. He ripped her panties right from her body, making Gloria cry out in pain at the stretch and tear of the fabric on her sore ass, and he brought his hand down hard on her pussy, giving her five good, hard slaps right to her cunt.

Gloria screamed, grabbing the pillow to hold over her face to muffle her cries. "Henry, why are you doing this?"

He moved the pillow from in front of her face, so that he was staring threateningly into her eyes as he said, "I'll stop when you quit lying to me."

She took a deep breath. "I was thinking about how many of the men I've fucked have been dominants. Only you, and one other."

"So, you were thinking about other men as you were sucking my cock, Gloria?"

"Baby, I—*fuck!*"

Five more hard slaps to her cunt, and Gloria was sobbing. Henry took the pillow and gently placed it over her face, then she felt him move down the bed, between her legs. She felt him blowing cool breaths against her stinging pussy lips, against her destroyed clit.

It *did* feel good, she thought...some sort of relief to the brutality she'd endured.

But she still cried. Two dominants among all the men she'd slept with, and she still thought she was a submissive? What if she was wrong? What if she was only with Henry because he had given her some sort of identity she wasn't even sure belonged to her?

She knew her fear-filled thoughts weren't the truth. In her heart, Gloria was certain she'd married Henry because he was the love of her life...no matter how difficult their marriage could be.

She knew from experience she could not live without him.

Seconds later, she felt him gently ease her folds apart. She gasped and whimpered at the still aching sting, but then his tongue brushed against her abused flesh...oh, my *god!*

Just as with her breasts, when Henry had slapped them earlier before fondling and playing with her nipples, her pussy was in a heightened state of being, every nerve ending on alert.

She felt every brush of Henry's tongue at a heightened amplitude, and it was the most exquisite pleasure she could have imagined. She moaned, her hips grinding against his face as he ate her, and that time, Henry didn't pin her down.

He feasted on her.

"Oh, god, baby, don't stop," she whimpered, tossing the pillow she'd screamed into aside so she could reach down, digging one hand into Henry's hair as she gently scraped her nails against his scalp, her other hand massaging his back as he ate her exquisitely.

“I knew you’d like that, babygirl,” he said, lapping his tongue all the way up her pussy, from her vaginal opening, to her very sensitive, stinging, red swollen clit, which he caught between his lips, teasing her as she panted.

Then his tongue assailed her sensitive bundle of nerves, and Gloria convulsed, her cunt pulsing as she came.

She hadn’t come down from the incredible high of her orgasm before Henry plunged his cock deep inside her still clenching pussy. She moaned, then screamed, as Henry grabbed her thighs and began hammering into her, furious and fast.

He moaned and panted as he fucked her. “I love your sweet pussy.”

“Henry, oh my god!”

"Fuck, baby," he muttered, lifting her ass so he could piston in and out of her at a quicker, more furious pace, hammering her so hard it hurt, but she loved every second of it.

Soon she was cumming again, dripping more of her own secretions onto Henry's cock buried deep inside her.

She moaned. "Henry, don't stop!"

"I won't," he said, fucking her harder.

Gloria wasn't sure how much more she could take without him quite literally breaking her, but seconds later, he grunted, shooting his hot cum deep inside her.

Gloria screamed again, and Henry silenced her cries with his mouth, kissing her deeply, his tongue mimicking what his cock had done to her moments earlier.

Slowly, they both came back down from their incredible highs. Henry rolled onto his side, holding her close to him. "Good girl."

She whimpered out a response. She was completely exhausted, more so than she could remember being after sex in a long time.

Henry cuddled her close, kissing the back of her neck, grabbing her hair and moving it over her shoulder so that he could work his mouth over her flesh.

"I love you so much, Henry," she whispered.

He reached forward, one hand to her front, as he began to soothingly fondle her breasts. "I love the way you touch me, baby."

His hand gave each nipple a tight pinch, and Gloria whimpered. He moved his hands down her body, over her belly, between her legs, where his fingers brushed against her sore, swollen clit.

She flinched, and Henry laughed softly, burying his face in her neck. "Too much, babygirl?"

"Hmm, right now, maybe," she whispered, reaching down and taking his hand in both of hers, bringing it back up to her face, where she began kissing and sucking his fingers, making him moan.

"You're making me hard again," he said.

She rolled over, smiling at him. "Well. I certainly won't stop you."

He took her at her word, rolling her onto her back as he began kissing her, slowly and deeply, running his fingers through her hair, climbing on top of her. She wrapped her legs around him as he lowered himself over her, as he spread her legs again.

She was so sore, from both the hot sex they'd just had *and* from the sex from that morning...it had been a long time since Gloria had been fucked that much in one day.

But Henry kissed her hard once more, then he moved away, getting into the bedside drawer, where he pulled out a bottle of lube and a butt plug.

Gloria swallowed. "Baby?"

"If your pussy is too sore, I can always fuck your ass again."

"Um..."

"You love it when I own your ass, Gloria." He leaned in over her, kissing her mouth. "You know you do, babygirl."

"Yes, Henry," she said.

She wasn't sure if she did or not, for that matter, but she supposed that, in some ways, it was easier for her to allow Henry to tell her what to think and who she was...although she knew it wasn't healthy.

She didn't care, though, as long as she made Henry happy. She was nervous about having anal sex again, especially if he intended to fuck her ass as hard as he'd fucked her face and her pussy.

Clearly, though, he fully intended to own all three of her holes as they fucked that day.

He squirted a generous amount of lube onto his fingers, then onto her asshole, making her gasp in shock at how cold the gel was.

He smiled as he began massaging the lube over her hole. "You'll be wishing for the cooling relief once I'm done with you, baby."

She swallowed hard as he then took the butt plug and coated it in lube. "I want you properly stretched and ready for me to take you," he explained.

She tried to prepare herself for the feeling of being split by the plug... It was one of her favorite toys, one she had chosen herself and had bought back when she had been single, after Donovan. It was cute, pink, and looked like a conversation heart at its end... she used it a lot back when she had first bought it.

She took a deep breath, and she saw Henry looking closely at her, seeing how worried she was. "Gloria, you know I won't hurt you."

"I know," she said, though she wasn't sure she believed it.

She knew Henry. She knew his tastes...he was going to do whatever he wanted, no matter how Gloria felt about it.

"Relax, babygirl," he said, and she felt the tip of the toy right at her tight anal opening.

She nodded, taking a deep breath and spreading her thighs more, so she was more opened to him.

He rubbed her inner thigh in gentle circles with one hand, while he pushed the toy inside her with the other.

Gloria gasped, then panted... the plug was too large, and the stretch was too much for her. "Henry," she gasped out.

"You're doing so *good*, baby," he told her, moving his fingers to her glistening pussy.

Henry began stroking her folds... she quickly found she was still incredibly sensitive from earlier. She began moaning and writhing in pleasure at Henry's gentle touch, which made the sting of the plug inside her tight asshole less painful. She smiled at Henry, softly and gratefully, and was rewarded by a soft—yet hungry—smile of his own, and she could tell he was more than ready to devour her.

He wasn't going to give her a gentle anal fuck.

He moved over her, squeezing her breasts and stroking her nipples erotically as he kissed her.

She kissed him back, absorbing his tender touch and kiss to use as a future balm to steel herself against the pain.

He finally positioned himself at her opening, quickly lubing himself up and removing the plug, immediately replacing it with his cock.

Gloria moaned and Henry thrust deeper, giving shallow pushes until he managed to make his way halfway inside her.

"God."

"You're so much better than I remembered, Gloria," he said rubbing her lower back, where he held onto her.

She could only whimper in response, her breathing shallow...it hurt so much, she wasn't sure she could take it, panting with his every thrust. He kept going, easing deeper and deeper.

"Henry, please go a bit easier on me."

He looked down at her face. Seeing the distress she was in, he kept going. Gloria wasn't naive. She knew her pain and discomfort brought him pleasure. It had from the beginning.

"It's okay, babygirl." He leaned up to press his lips against hers, then said, "You know how much I love you?"

"Yes, Henry."

He kissed her lips once more, then pulled back, tasting her breasts as he worked down her body, then Gloria gave a startled yelp as Henry dragged her down the bed until her ass was hanging over its edge. Henry used her position to his advantage, beginning to thrust harder and deeper inside her, making her moans of pleasure turn to cries of pain.

"Henry," she pleaded.

He began to slam his cock inside her asshole more ruthlessly, deeming her ready for him.

Gloria screamed as he got progressively rougher and rougher, then as he grabbed her legs and lifted them above her head, making her asshole tighter, the sex more painful for her as Henry's pleasure increased.

"Ugh, fuck! I love your tight little hole."

Gloria felt like he was tearing out her insides. She couldn't protest, too breathless from trying to endure.

She longed for the gentle, passionate lovemaking from that morning, but she was beginning to realize anew that the only way she was getting loving, tender sex from him was if he got to brutalize her in turn.

He started pumping and pumping her as hard as he humanly could.

Finally, he came hard, and Gloria could feel his hot spunk gush up inside her bowels. She moaned—mostly in discomfort—and he remained inside her, flipping her onto her side as he moved up the bed, spooning her.

She longed to feel the relief of his cock leaving her asshole.

He stroked her hair and down her back... she was in too much pain from the unwelcome stretch of her ass to notice whether he was softening inside her.

He brushed her blond curls aside, kissing her. "I love you, Gloria."

She closed her eyes. "I love you, too. Baby..."

"What?" he asked, still running his fingers through her hair and sensually kissing her neck, tasting her.

"Can you pull out? It's really hurting me."

"Yes."

He did, and she flinched as his thick, bulbous head painfully tore at her again before she finally managed to find some relief.

She sighed.

Henry fondled her breasts affectionately in his afterglow... while Gloria was simply sweating.

"Thanks," he said. "I needed that."

She gingerly rolled over, remaining in his arms and curling up close to him.

"Are you feeling better?"

He blew out his breath. "I mean, I was feeling alright before, babygirl."

"Henry..."

"What is it?" he asked, placing a finger underneath her chin and lifting her face to meet his gaze.

She took a deep breath, knowing that she was taking a huge leap, opening herself up to all kinds of suffering as she asked, "Henry, are you happy? I mean, genuinely."

"What do you mean? With you, or in general?"

She let out a shaky breath. "Both, baby."

"I'm not sure."

Gloria swallowed hard, nodding... It was heartbreaking for her, thinking that—despite everything that she had done, how much she had endured, for *him*—she might genuinely not make him happy.

“Babygirl, I don’t mean to hurt you. But I promised—”

“That you will always be honest with me,” Gloria repeated that same phrase that he had spoken to her on numerous occasions throughout their relationship...she knew what she could count on from him.

He was always going to—*consistently*—hurt her.

And no matter how hard she tried for him, he was never going to be completely happy with her.

Acknowledging that fact broke her.

3

Chapter Three

Henry could tell how badly he'd hurt Gloria; the question was whether he cared or not. Gloria's suspicions were that he, in fact, did not.

But she turned away from him…not in anger, which would have been easier to deal with, but in hurt. Using the same pillow that had muffled her screams and cries of ecstasy earlier to hide her sobs.

“This is why I hate being honest. I hate seeing you cry.”

“You love it when I cry.”

He barely heard her words through the muffle of the pillow. “I don’t.”

“During sex.”

“That’s different,” he said, his fingers beginning to stroke her back.

She only cried harder.

He hugged her. “Was I that rough? Did I hurt you *that* badly?”

“You always do,” she said. “I’m crying because I don’t make you happy…all of *this* isn’t enough to make you fucking happy.”

Henry flipped her over onto her back, brushing the tears from her cheeks before kissing her lips softly.

She wondered how he could kiss her and touch her so tenderly when he’d made it clear how unhappy he was.

“What can I do?” he asked. “I can’t stand to see you like this.”

She shook her head. “Just don’t leave me.”

“I won’t leave you.” He kissed her forehead. “Not ever.”

“Can you just…”

Knowing she was going to ask to be held, Henry wrapped his arms around her and pulled her close. “No strings attached, I’m here to hold you as long as you need me to. Or, until the babies wake.”

She laughed, then turned toward him, burying her face against him, stroking his soft chest hair. “Baby...we need to work through some things.”

“We will.”

“I can't lose what...what we once had,” Gloria whispered.

“We haven’t lost anything. We’ve gained three beautiful additions to what we had. We’re doing well, babygirl...” he took a long, careful look at her. “I can see, though, I might not be the only one who isn’t happy.”

“Henry, I **am** happy with you as my husband.” She hesitated, biting her lip. “I won’t lie...some of the things you do make me unhappy, but it’s not you. I love you, baby, and nothing will ever change that. I mean...look at all I’ve sacrificed for you. Nothing will change how I feel.”

He stared deeply at her all throughout her speech, then said, “Tell me what I *can* do to make you happier.”

“Come home and sleep in our bed at night.”

“Gloria.”

“I’m being honest,” she said, throwing his words back at him.

“I see.” He sighed. “I’ll try to do better. Sometimes I need an escape from all of this.”

Gloria sat up, ignoring the pain she was in and her nudity. “Did you leave Vic at home with the babies all night while you were out drinking, Henry?”

He frowned. “Things were different back then. We were so young...Vic couldn’t have done it without me.”

“Or you loved her more than you love me,” Gloria whispered, knowing she would cause an argument, but those words had been choking her.

“No,” he said. “She was so young, and she’d never done anything like that before—”

“I might not be twenty like you all were when you started your family,” Gloria said, “but I’ve never had a baby before, either. And now I’ve got three. I can barely keep my head above water most days, Henry. I *need* you here with me.”

He stared at her for a long moment, then he leaned forward and softly began stroking her naked breasts.

“I don’t like how you’re raising Eva,” he said, still fondling her.

“I can’t say ‘no’ to her.”

Henry shook his head.

“How can *you* tell her?” Gloria demanded. “Looking into that sweet, adorable face, and denying her anything she wants?”

"Because, Gloria, I have three other children and I've done this before. You're teaching her that she can have whatever she wants, and that's not the right way to bring up a child."

"Doesn't she *deserve* to have everything she wants?" Gloria asked.

He laughed, drawing her close and hugging her fiercely. "Babygirl, you're impossible to argue with...just as you're impossible to please. You and Eva are one and the same. Both spoiled princesses who expect to be worshipped."

She frowned at him.

He kissed her cheek. "I knew what I was getting into when I married you, Gloria Titus."

She curled into him. "As long as you're okay with it."

He kissed her neck. "Baby, I'll try to be home from now on no later than midnight...well, one a.m. Okay?"

She knew it was the most he was willing to give her...for the time being.

"Are you gonna be okay, babygirl?" Henry asked.

"Just please understand that I love our babies more than anything...but I've sacrificed it *all* for you. Sometimes I feel like you forget that."

"I'm sorry," he said, seeming sincere.

She kissed his lips, softly and tenderly. "I need to be held, comforted, and reassured. *You did know* when you married me how high-maintenance I am."

"And I've always loved you for it," he whispered sexily, kissing her neck again.

"I need more of you," she said.

"I'll do better."

He held her a few more moments, then they could both tell that the babies had awakened, from the sounds coming through the monitor.

Henry surprised her by saying, "I've got this. Take your time, take a nice bath, and I'll watch them while you do what you need to do."

Gloria hesitated. "Are you sure?"

"Better go before I change my mind," he said, smiling at her.

Gloria wrapped her arms around him and held him close, kissing him passionately before she released her hold on him, taking him at his word and hurrying to the massive ensuite bathroom.

Gloria was already naked. She looked at herself in the mirror...her bruises were already showing. She was certain her ass would be sore for ages. Gloria had some light bruising already around her nipples and the upper part of her breasts.

She wanted to take a bath, but since she was covered in sweat and cum, she decided to take a quick shower first, to rinse off before she ran her bath and soaked her sore ass and pussy.

She reached into the shower and started the water...it warmed almost immediately, but she checked out the quickly forming bruises on her ass before she stepped into the shower, closing the doors behind her before she could focus on how terrible she was going to end up looking within the hour.

It had been a long time since she'd seen the effects of her and Henry's lifestyle written all over her body.

After showering, Gloria slid into her bath, allowing the hot water to envelop her...it hurt, the hot water against her aching, stinging privates, but soon the sting was overpowered by the delicious feel of the water soaking her sore muscles.

She sighed, wishing she could force herself to relax, to think about nothing for once.

She could have stayed in the tub all night, but she forced herself to get out, wincing in pain as she climbed out of the tub.

She dried and applied lotion carefully, gently massaging it into her tender, red flesh before she wrapped in her silk robe and went back into the bedroom, then to her own walk-in closet (Henry's closet was on the other end of the ensuite bathroom, through another door, and while it was still a large closet, it was nothing like the massive, elaborate closet that Gloria housed her own clothing in), directly across their bedroom from the bathroom.

There was a balcony both in the bedroom *and* in her closet, but most of the time, it was either too hot, too cold, or too rainy in London for them to regularly enjoy the outdoors.

Gloria went to the back quarter section of her closet, closest to the window overlooking their little side yard, which was basically invisible from where she stood, as she rifled through the silk padded, pink hangers holding her lounge clothes.

Gloria selected a lace bralette and lace panties to match, then some black leggings and a soft sweatshirt, slipping her feet into thick wool socks to keep her warm.

Finally, Gloria felt ready to get on her chores...first finishing the laundry and washing their sheets before she went to cook dinner.

Gloria had never enjoyed cooking, and only learned how to do so when she had children, wanting to be able to cook them nice, healthy meals.

She started chopping vegetables. She was going to prepare a salad, chopped steak for Henry, along with roasted vegetables, and roasted Portobello mushroom with her vegetables, rather than steak, since she'd been a vegetarian since she was fifteen...well over half her life.

For the babies, she had chopped up vegetables and had steamed them on the stove, while her and Henry's food cooked in the oven.

Gloria also grilled some chicken strips for Eva... the twins were too small yet to eat chicken, but she grilled one strip to split between them, trying to expose them to more foods, as she pureed more fruit for them to go along with their vegetables.

She filled the plates with pureed fruit and vegetables for the twins, vegetables and chicken for Eva while her and Henry's dinner finished cooking.

She and Henry started to feed the babies. Once they were settled and eating, she said, "I'll be back, I need to put some laundry in, then I'll finish cooking our dinner."

"Not that we will get to eat much," he said.

She stared at him, then shrugged. "I suppose."

Soon her sheets were in the dryer. She tossed most of the laundry into the hamper to fold later, hanging up what could wrinkle, as the timer on the oven went off.

She pulled out her and Henry's dinner, then prepared their salad plates, setting them down on the table before going to fill glasses of water for them both.

When she returned to the table and set Henry's water glass in front of him, he looked up at her. "A beer, babygirl?"

She chewed her lip. "Are you sure that's a good idea?"

"Are you going to sit down and help me feed them?" Henry asked.

She nodded, going back to the kitchen with her and Henry's plates. She took over feeding the twins as she found Henry getting close to arguing with Eva.

'Oh, no,' Gloria thought...

"You're not getting a biscuit."

"But mummy told me—"

"I don't care what she told you. Now, eat your dinner, Eva."

Eva looked pitifully up at her mother. "Mummy..."

"Baby—"

But then Eva burst into tears. Gloria sighed, and Eva jumped down off her booster seat and ran to jump into Gloria's lap.

"Darling, it's okay," Gloria said, stroking her back soothingly as she did her best to try to also feed Cheye, who held her mouth open expectantly, wanting her next bite of dinner.

Henry frowned, pushing back his chair and standing up, grabbing Eva out of Gloria's lap. "Come, your mother is busy."

Eva screeched in protest. "No! Mummy!"

Gloria swallowed hard... she would have burst into tears, if she hadn't been about to laugh from the twins's antics as they regarded their older sister as though she were from another planet, then glanced at each other before they looked expectantly at their mother to feed them.

But Gloria was concerned for Eva... Henry had taken her to the living room, which she could see from the kitchen, but she knew how short Henry's temper could be.

"Henry!"

"What, Gloria?" he demanded.

Gloria swallowed. "Just bring her back. It's quite okay, I'll deal with it."

He glanced at her sharply. "Absolutely not, Gloria. You can't handle anything when it comes to Eva."

"Henry, bring her back here, now."

He stared at her... even Eva stopped crying.

The only two making any sort of racket were Cheye and Jem, whining a bit in their hunger and want for their dinner.

Henry brought Eva back into the dining room, sitting her in her booster seat.

"Will you eat your dinner for Mummy?" Gloria asked, smiling softly at her oldest daughter, still such a sweet baby, above all else... she was sensitive.

Like her mother.

Eva kept crying, but picked up a tiny chunk of chicken and stuck it in her mouth, more interested in playing with her utensils than she was in eating.

Gloria quietly fed the twins. Henry picked at his dinner... Gloria could tell that he was upset.

With her, no doubt.

They finished dinner, and Gloria took the twins for their bath... telling Eva to come along to help.

She knew she was pissing Henry off, but she was afraid to leave Eva alone with him. It wasn't that she was afraid Henry would hurt Eva...

Considering the mood he was in, though, it was possible. He could hurt *her,* after all.

"I'll clean up," Henry said.

"Thank you," Gloria threw over her shoulder, trying to detect any hint of anger or irritation in Henry's tone.

She was nervous about what that night would be like, wondering if he'd take his frustrations out on her, or if he'd discipline her for going against him.

She got her babies all washed up and into their pajamas; she wasn't sure what she was going to do when they started school and she had to help them with their homework on top of everything else.

Eva went to sit on the sofa...she wanted to watch *Bluey*, but she always did put up a fight in the evenings, when it came to wanting to do what she wanted to do, rather than following what Gloria had been trying so hard to make into her routine...

"*Bluey,* Mummy?"

"Baby, I'm—"

"You're not watching *Bluey*, Eva. Not until you start behaving better."

Eva didn't understand her Daddy's words, but she started crying...she understood the word 'no,' even if she didn't hear it all that often.

Gloria supposed she would find out later that night *exactly* how Henry had felt about everything that had happened that day.

Gloria herself was feeling beyond overwhelmed, and entirely defeated.

It was around eight that evening when they finally had the babies in bed...which was typically around the time that Henry would fuck off to the bar, and Gloria would be left alone all evening. It should have been the perfect time for her to work on her novel, but she typically worked until nine or ten to get the house cleaned and laundry finished. She would be too exhausted by that time to even pull her laptop out, much less to write a novel.

At that point, she knew that she may as well have simply started over...or perhaps it was that she should have given up entirely, based off how the rest of her life was going.

But Henry hadn't changed for the pub...in fact, when she came in from the girls' rooms, he was sitting at the dining room table, his head in his hands.

Gloria took a deep breath. "Henry?"

"Come have a seat, babygirl."

She made her way to the dining room, pulling out the seat directly across from her husband.

"No."

Gloria hesitated.

"Come, sit closer."

Still uncertain, Gloria took the seat beside Henry.

"Gloria."

She met his eyes.

Henry frowned as he looked at her. "May I ask why you're acting as though you are afraid of me?"

"I just...I thought you were upset with me?"

She wasn't sure why her statement came out sounding like a question...residual regret from earlier that morning, she supposed.

Heaven help her, it had been a long-ass day.

"I'm upset, but there's no reason for you to be afraid, Gloria. What do you think that I'm going to do to you?"

"I...I'm not sure," she whispered.

"Have I ever hit you?"

Gloria chewed her lip.

He leveled his gaze with hers. "Have I ever hit you when we weren't playing, Gloria?"

"No."

"Gloria."

"Yes, Henry?"

"We aren't in our dynamic right now. I'm speaking to you as my equal."

She looked curiously at him...he'd never spoken so directly, clearly defining the parameters of their dynamic...or, if he had, it had been so long ago that Gloria couldn't recall.

“I need to know if you genuinely believe I would put a hand on our child.”

She shook her head. “I don’t think you would.”

“I thought we’d worked past what happened this morning. I know I hurt you.”

“I’m fine.”

“Can you really handle this?” Henry asked.

She nodded.

“I need you to speak the words, babygirl.”

“I can handle anything you want us to do, Henry.”

“Tell me where we go from here. Because I’m stressed out, and I know you are, too. I need you to tell me exactly what it is that has you on edge. Besides being afraid of me.”

“Henry, I’m not.”

“Speak to me,” he repeated, in a serious tone offering no room for argument.

"I need some help," she finally admitted. "I can't do all the housework and childcare on my own. Baby, I know you help...I want to get back to writing, and I can't do that unless you take over more of the work around the house."

She'd been so afraid to speak those words to him, but as soon as they were out, she knew there was no going back...no reversing what had been spoken.

Just as with earlier that morning and asking him if he was having an affair, it was too late to go back.

"I do help out, Gloria."

"If I'm going to write, I'll need you to get up with them in the mornings, and to take over everything around the house. I know that's asking a lot, but if you want to keep up this lifestyle, we're going to have to make some changes. I've got to get back to work, Henry."

4

Chapter Four

"Thank you for coming on such short notice," Gloria told her mother, as Mrs. Alexander came to pick the children up to take to her own flat...which was in the same building as Gloria and Henry's home.

She knew that Gloria's mother and father had argued over the flat...and she also knew that the main argument had been that they hadn't bought the most expensive flat in the building. Gloria had, with the money from her writing career, which was a thorn in her father's side.

Gloria knew her own father resented Mrs. Alexander coming to England, although she came to see her grandchildren. Gloria's father hadn't spoken to her since she'd moved to England the *first* time, and he'd never even seen his granddaughters...even more reason why he was as good as dead, as far as Gloria was concerned.

"I'll take any excuse to see my grandchildren," Gloria's mother said, smiling at Eva as she picked her up.

Gloria watched her mother and her daughter together, her heart melting...it was moments like this that made her question why she had thought it a good idea to start a family across the ocean from her mother.

But she had no regrets, truly. She loved London, and she loved Henry.

End of discussion.

Henry stood beside Gloria, wrapping his arm around her shoulder. "We appreciate the help."

"Not a problem. I'm happy to help," Gloria's mother replied, holding Eva against her chest as the child rested her head on her grandmother.

"So, six tomorrow evening?" Gloria asked, leaning into Henry's embrace.

She felt guilty for asking her mother to watch the babies all on her own...heaven knew Gloria was well aware of just how much work three babies on her own were.

But she also needed her mother's help more than she was comfortable admitting. She and Henry needed to get their acts together, and Gloria needed to start writing again.

"Yes, that's wonderful, dear."

"If you need anything, either call or just come by, okay?" Gloria asked.

Henry gave her side a pinch, but she did her best not to react...her mother already didn't like him. The last thing Gloria needed was for her mother to have one more reason to hate her husband.

"That won't be necessary," Mrs. Alexander said as she carried Eva inside.

Henry had the twins in their carriers; he picked them up and brought them into the flat, following Gloria's mother, as Gloria bent and hefted the two overflowing diaper bags inside.

Once the babies were settled, Gloria and Henry told them goodnight. Eva hugged Gloria goodbye, but she didn't seem too torn up about being away from her mother for the night.

Finally, Gloria and Henry headed up to their own suite. They took the elevator upstairs, and on the way there, Henry turned toward her, grabbing her ass and shoving her against the wall.

"What are you doing?" she asked, breathless.

"Not wasting any time."

She moaned as his mouth found hers, kissing her long and hard, his hands kneading her butt cheeks. He pulled her dress up, sticking his hand down her leggings, inside her panties...

Seconds later, Gloria felt his fingers brushing against her quickly swelling and dripping pussy.

"Henry," she moaned.

"Get on your knees."

She immediately dropped to her knees, looking up at him.

"Unzip my trousers and suck my cock, babygirl."

She took a deep breath, biting her lip hard. She was practically panting as she took his hard cock out of his trousers and held his gaze as she ran her tongue along his head.

He moaned. "That *mouth*, babygirl."

She took him deeper into her mouth, sucking him hard, not wasting any time since they had less than a minute before the elevator would reach the penthouse.

She sucked him furiously, and he moaned and thrust into her mouth, holding the back of her head as he guided her mouth right where he wanted her.

She stopped before the elevator opened into the penthouse. He kept his hand on the back of her neck as she rose to her feet, never breaking eye contact.

He backed her into the living room, and as the elevator doors closed behind them, he whipped her around so her back was to his front.

He closed his fingers around her throat as he reached into the front of her leggings, his hands back inside her panties as he teased her folds.

She moaned. "Fuck."

He pressed his mouth against her neck. "That's exactly what I'm going to do to you, babygirl."

Gloria gasped as he ripped her tights and panties right off her body. She stood naked from the waist down in their foyer, her tight bodycon red dress bunched around her waist as Henry got to his knees beneath her and began eating her.

“Holy fuck, Henry!”

“Sit on my face,” he ordered. “Now.”

It wasn't a demand Gloria needed to hear twice; she immediately sank to her knees, straddling his face as his tongue drank her in. He had her trembling and convulsing in moments as he held her thighs firmly to keep her upright.

She still fell forward, but Henry only gave her a second or two of recovery before he pried her off the floor, holding her in his arms as he carried her to the dining room table, the very place where they had their family dinners. As he lay her back across the table, her ass hanging off, before he slipped his cock right inside her dripping pussy.

Gloria whimpered as he fucked her, his cock buried so deep inside her that he *had* to be against her cervix as he held himself there, twisting his hips from side to side, stretching her.

Gloria gasped at the beyond exquisite feeling of her husband buried so deep inside her, as his cock began to twitch in pleasure at the feel of her walls clamping down on him.

He began rubbing her clit with his thumb, sending Gloria over the edge as she came hard, exploding with pleasure as her orgasm overtook her, as it kept rolling as he continued fucking her slow, gentle, and deep, still circling her clit with hard presses.

She gasped and panted, thrashing across the table...she didn’t think she could handle anything more.

“Babygirl, you’re going to have to stay still—”

"*Fuck,*" Gloria moaned, "I...I *can't!*"

She involuntarily came so hard she bucked Henry off her, then she crashed hard to the marble floor below.

"Fuck," Henry muttered, "are you hurt, baby?"

Gloria was still twitching and cumming. She couldn't respond right away, still gasping for breath.

"Baby?" he repeated.

"I'm going to have bruises and I'll be sore. I'm okay though."

He helped her to her feet. "I've never seen anyone cum that hard."

Her knees were still weak and shaking. She clung to Henry, unable to walk straight, and he ended up picking her up and carrying her to their bedroom.

"I don't want you to do anything strenuous the rest of the night...I'm afraid you're hurt."

"You've not gotten off yet," she said.

"Well, babygirl...you want to suck my cock?"

She moaned softly, seeing how hard he was as he stuck out of his trousers.

She started to reach out to take his cock in her hand, but he grabbed both her wrists.

"Get at the foot of the bed."

"Yes, Henry."

Henry came around the bed, sitting down, his cock in her face, ready for her.

She started sucking him deep, him fucking her face. Gloria could feel his desperation to get off, to blow his load down her throat, to find his enormous relief.

"On your knees, lean forward with your ass in the air," Henry demanded, grabbing her ass cheeks and spreading them hard, as his cock was shoved down her throat by her new position.

He put one hand behind the back of her neck, shoving his cock balls deep down her throat.

He came hard, groaning, and Gloria moaned around his cock. She held him there until he eased out of her mouth.

"On the bed."

She got on their bed, on her hands and knees...not sure what he wanted, but assuming his favorite position to take her in.

He slapped her ass.

She gasped and whimpered, then shrieked in pain as he kept slapping her red and raw. She thought he'd never stop hitting her, and sighed in relief when he finally *did* stop.

"On your back now, babygirl," Henry said.

Obediently Gloria rolled over onto her back, spreading her legs as she looked up into his face...she took a deep breath, her ass stinging, but she was ready for whatever he did next.

“I want you to suck my cock again, Gloria,” he said, moving up the bed so that his crotch was in her face.

“Yes, Henry.”

She reached out and took his cock in her hands...then began working her tongue underneath, teasing him, stopping just before she licked the underside of his head.

She went back to long strokes against the underside of his shaft, her eyes never leaving his...she could see the frustration in his eyes.

“Gloria, get your lips around my cock, *now,* ”he demanded.

She moaned, then pulled his head between her lips, tightening them around that sensitive part of his cock...before she teasingly, again, allowed him to pop out of her mouth as she cupped his balls and began lapping at the underside of his cock, yet again...

Gloria wasn’t expecting what he did next...she’d thought Henry would never be able to surprise her...

...but she’d been wrong.

He moved his hand back to slap her. She'd expected a pussy slap, and was kind of looking forward to it, but instead, he did the unimaginable, slapping her—*hard*—across the face.

Instantly, Gloria flipped out, starting to cry. "Fuck!"

Henry slapped her again before she could think straight enough to say her safe word...

"Red!" she screamed, bursting into tears again.

Henry instantly stopped. He stepped back off the bed, pulling his trousers on as Gloria curled in on herself, crying.

"Gloria, are you okay?"

"No! I told you to never do that," she sobbed, forcing herself to roll onto her side so that she could look him in the face.

"You're being dramatic."

"No, I'm *not!"* she insisted. "Henry, you know better than that."

"I *know* better?" he demanded.

"It's one of my hard limits, and you knew that!" She kept crying, unable to rein in her emotions.

She'd never thought she'd have to protect herself from her husband, the man who was supposed to love her and protect her.

"And then you cry so that I can't be angry with you," he said, sounding disgusted.

Gloria was not only hurt, but also confused...she didn't understand how Henry could be angry with her, at all, for using her safe word...it brought her right back to when their relationship had first begun, when she'd been afraid if she told him 'no' to anything, he'd break up with her.

After all, he'd plainly told her that he could easily replace her. He'd been lying, but Gloria hadn't known it at the time, and it had been unfair of him to speak to her that way in the first place. She only cried harder...after everything that the two of them had been through together, he was *still* bullying her.

He still saw her as an object.

But, as always, the second that she truly began to see that he was using her and that he was a cruel son-of-a-bitch, she felt him climb onto the bed beside her, wrapping his arms around her.

"Hey," he said, tenderly stroking her back. "Babygirl, I'm sorry. I'm sorry I hit you, and I'm sorry I made you cry."

She took a deep breath, then forced herself to roll over to face him. "Are you?"

"Very," he said, wrapping his arms around her, pulling her close.

She didn't protest or try to pull away. Gloria allowed Henry to hold her, then his lips found hers, working against her mouth.

"I love you so much, Gloria," he said, easing his lips down to her neck.

"I love you, too."

He moved his hand from her back, down to her ass, gently stroking her blistered skin. "I won't ever hurt you."

She pulled back, her hands on his face.

"Nothing more than what we agreed upon...which won't ever truly hurt you."

"I trust you, Henry...which is why this is so difficult for me. I trusted you to *never* violate my hard limits."

He placed his hand on the back of her head, working his fingers through her hair. "I know."

"Don't ever hit me again, please," she whispered.

He kissed her forehead, holding her close. "I promise."

Perhaps Gloria should have been a little harder on him, should have expected more of him, but at the same time, she felt herself softening. She knew she was too tender for her own good, too forgiving, but she was too in love with Henry *not* to be.

Slowly, he began exploring her body with his hands. His touch was gentle and loving, knowing there was no way Gloria would stand for anything rough or remotely BDSM...not after what she'd gone through at his hands, moments before.

Perhaps it was unsatisfactory sex for him, but he knew he had a duty to give Gloria what she needed in those moments.

He slowly, thoroughly turned her on, making sure she was dripping wet and wanting before he began making love to her...sweet, loving, gentle sex, giving Gloria slow, long, rolling orgasms all throughout the night.

As the two lovers finally lay—close to sleep, absolutely spent from their long night of soft pleasure—Gloria couldn't find sleep right away, although Henry was deeply asleep within a few moments.

She knew that—no matter how apologetic he had been toward her for his earlier actions, and no matter how good their makeup had been—he was going to want to go at her hard again, likely before she'd fully recovered from the trauma he'd caused her.

She was going to have to pay.

It wasn't over.

5

Chapter Five

The next morning, Gloria left Henry in bed as she grabbed her laptop and headed for her home office, determined to get some writing in before Henry woke... she wasn't sure what he had in mind for their day, but she had the feeling he would want her focus and attention on him, rather than on her all but abandoned novel.

Gloria hadn't sat at her writing desk in ages. She hadn't opened a Word document in months, discouraged from finding herself too exhausted or stressed about the fact that she hadn't written a book in so long to be able to focus on writing.

It was a miserable position for an author to find herself in, with so much to say—so many rich, evocative emotions to convey through her stories—but no time or energy to put those stories to paper...or word processor, in Gloria's case.

But as she opened her Word document, Gloria was more determined than ever to write. She noted the time; it was still early. She doubted Henry would be awake for some time, and since Gloria's mother had taken the babies, it meant she had several uninterrupted hours to get down to writing the story she was dying to tell.

It was bliss unheard of...Gloria's second biggest fear—or maybe third—about having children was that she wouldn't have time to write anymore, as writing had been Gloria's saving grace throughout the years. She needed it. Once her babies were in the world, her fear of never getting to write had become a reality.

Thank heavens Gloria's mother had agreed to come to London for a while, giving Gloria a much-needed break. Otherwise, she never would have touched her book again. It was thus—Gloria realizing just how lucky she truly was—that her fingers brushed against the keyboard...

And the magic of writing ensued, consuming the next few hours of Gloria's life, in which she was finally able to serve her purpose.

It was noon before Gloria knew it.

She'd been so caught up in her writing that time had truly slipped away, but the twinge in her back and her slight headache from staring at her screen for hours reminded her.

And it literally *had* been hours... Gloria had sat with her cup of tea and her laptop around seven that morning, so she'd gotten in five-plus hours of solid, interrupted writing time.

While Gloria had been focused on writing, the sun had risen behind her back, displaying a gorgeous view of London behind her as the city had come to life, rush hour had passed, and now the day was progressing at its pace many stories below her.

She realized, after having taken a break to stretch and staring at the city below, that she rarely had time anymore to appreciate the beauty of London. Not from the penthouse, nor especially from street level, as Gloria rarely left her home. It was one more of the little things Gloria's busy life left her little time for: enjoying the small pleasure of a gorgeous view of the famous city surrounding her.

Gloria wandered back to her desk, deciding to check some social media sites since she was already in the zone. She thought she might be ready to speak up about her new book. She mostly stayed off social media, being too busy with three small babies, but also because her readers had been hounding Gloria about her next book since she'd first announced it.

That announcement was nearly three years ago.

She couldn't blame them for getting antsy. At the same time, Gloria's anxiety was unbearable on her best days.

The pressure of putting her new book out into the world was almost more than she could take, but since she'd actually made some decent progress for the first time in ages, Gloria decided—perhaps foolishly—she should give her fans an update.

With trepidation, Gloria typed out her update:

Finally sat down to write this morning...5 hours of solid writing. Feeling alive again.

She stared at the words she had typed, working over them repeatedly in her head, trying to decide if she should press send, if anything she said could be misconstrued to make her look bad.

Gloria had to ask herself, however, how writing an update to her followers required more revisions, editing, and overthinking than writing the actual book.

Finally deeming her message to her readers acceptable, Gloria sighed, pressing "send" and then burying her face in her hands...too late to take it back now. Once something was posted on the Internet, it was there forever. In the age of screenshots and screen recordings, even *those* could be edited to falsify a narrative in order to defame somebody, as Gloria knew firsthand.

Although those bots when she first began publishing her erotica had been her family, a fact making the betrayal sting all the worse.

Gloria laid those negative thoughts to rest, knowing it did no good to dwell on things that had hurt her in the past. Her present and future were bright, and *that* was what was important.

Gloria smiled as the positive replies to her post quickly rolled in… followed by some not so positive responses.

Hi, I can't wait! You're my favorite author.

Yes! More smutty smut!

Again, no one cares anymore. So it took you four years almost to spend five hours writing. Congrats, you're old news.

THOT.

Gloria still wasn't sure if THOT was a compliment or an insult…she couldn't even be that upset over the other negative messages, since those were precisely the words the voice of imposter syndrome spoke to her.

She was about to shut down her laptop—hopefully it would not remain dormant as long as it had the last time—but then she saw a notification for a message from someone she'd never spoken to before, although they were mutual follows.

Gloria opened her messenger app and clicked on the unopened envelope icon to read the message.

Hi Gloria. I've been following your account for a while. I'm happy to see that you're back to writing again. I recently took a break, as I do each year, and I'll probably be starting back after the new year. Do you have any advice for me getting back into it?

Gloria chewed her lip. She always found it sweet when someone messaged her about writing, especially when asking for writing tips. However, she was always wary of men messaging her. She was married, for one thing; she also had men who messaged her at *first* asking for advice, and once they saw she'd message them back, their responses turned sexual.

Gloria had gotten her share of sexual messages online; to be fair, it was how she met her husband, but most of those men were nothing more than shitheads. Her own husband was a shithead.

He always had been.

Gloria had far less patience for men now she was a married woman with a family. She hated to admit it, but when she had been lonely and between lovers in the past, she'd entertained attention from some of those men...those who had bought fifty thousand plus followers and acted like they were doing her a favor by talking to her.

Those who could barely form cohesive sentences while messaging her...and even when she was sexting with them, they still hadn't promoted her books.

Again, though, pains from her past were now irrelevant. After all, her follower count trumped even the most "famous" of those men she'd spoken to, and she'd bought the most luxurious penthouse in her area of London with the money she'd earned from her books, with plenty still in the bank.

Truly, Gloria had nothing to be bitter about.

Even still, she wasn't sure how to respond to this man who messaged her. His intentions seemed pure, but then again, when it came down to it, Gloria wasn't naive.

A man's intentions with a woman were rarely pure.

Still Gloria didn't have much to do until Henry woke. She decided to message back, being friendly without being overly so, and making it subtly—yet abundantly—clear she was married.

She messaged this "Dean" back:

Sometimes a break is a good thing, because you come back stronger for it. It's a challenge to find time to write as a mother of three babies, even with the help of my husband (he hadn't helped all that much as of late, but Dean didn't need to know that).

I would say, start back by rereading the last thing that you wrote. It also always helps me to make a thorough outline of what I'm about to write. Hopefully this helps you. Best of luck!

Gloria thought her response would be the end of their conversation. As much as she hated to, she did have to leave some messages from her fans on read, or unopened. She didn't have enough hours in her day.

She was—yet again—about to shut her laptop down when she saw a new message in her inbox.

She sighed, deciding she had time for one more message before she shut her laptop down and went to put on some coffee, to make herself another cup of tea, and to cook a luxuriant brunch for Henry and herself.

She was surprised to see another message from Dean. She wanted their conversation to be done.

Thanks for the advice! You see, I take off several months a year for my girlfriend, but I've had a rough year this year, and I'm beginning to doubt my abilities. I'm worried I won't have it in me to get back to writing again.

Gloria decided to give him a quick, sterile reply, then to get offline quickly, which was a cowardly tactic, but she *was* a bit of a coward when it came to dealing socially with other people, even online.

She had to end this conversation with the random internet man, and fast...she knew Henry would be waking at any time, and there was a lot she wanted to do before he woke.

Well, I'm sure that you'll figure it out. Good luck, and Happy Holidays!

Gloria typed, then she immediately closed out of her social media account and made sure all her work had been backed up to her multiple cloud drives before she shut down her laptop, grabbed her mug, and headed down the hallway to the kitchen, where she quickly put on a pot of coffee for her husband, and started another pot of water boiling on the stove for her tea.

She gathered the ingredients she'd need, and she began mixing homemade pancake batter, adding fresh fruit (as fresh as one could buy during winter in London) to two different batches, strawberries to one and blueberries to another.

One thing Gloria desperately missed about her home in the United States was the Southern California produce...she almost loved it more than she loved Henry.

She was dropping spoonfuls of batter into the sizzling skillet when she felt strong arms wrap around her waist. Gloria moaned softly, leaning her head back against Henry's shoulder as he held her.

He kissed her neck. "I smelled coffee. I woke, and my beautiful wife wasn't in bed beside me."

"I wanted to surprise you with breakfast." She smiled, sighing happily as he nipped at the delicate skin of her neck. "Mmm," she whimpered as he began licking her, "that feels amazing."

She turned, wrapping her arms around him, looking up into his eyes. He placed his hand against her neck, brought her face close to his, and he kissed her, long, hard, and deep.

She smiled against his lips. "I was just thinking about how very much I love you."

He pulled back, holding her face in his hands, kissing her forehead. "Were you, baby-girl?"

She nodded. "Actually...how I wished you were my first."

"That's sweet," he said, pulling her tightly against him...

...causing Gloria to flinch in pain.

"Shit, I forgot you took a tumble last night, off of the dining room table no less."

"We need to shop for more rugs for the house. That really did hurt...I don't want the twins to get hurt when they start walking."

Henry's hands became gentle against her hips and back. "I'm sorry you got hurt."

She smiled. "Last night was worth it, baby."

He kissed her again, then went to make his cup of coffee as Gloria finished cooking breakfast.

Soon, the two of them were seated at their dining room table...the very one where Henry had made dessert of her pussy the night before.

“I think I'm going to feel shy eating at this table for a while."

Henry smiled deviously. "I was thinking we should have dinner with your mother here, and that she should sit right where your ass sat as I fucked you."

Gloria felt her face get hot, and she busied herself with her Earl Grey tea, stirring it obsessively.

"Babygirl, you're not getting shy on me, are you?"

She chewed her lip. "No, no, I'm just...she's my mother, Henry."

"And you got your looks from her."

She gave him a look of warning. "Stop it.”

"I love you. I want to fuck you senseless."

She laughed. "You always do, don't you?"

He gave her a dark, hungry look that made her pussy tingle deliciously. "And I know you need it just as badly."

She set down her fork. "You're my weakness, Henry."

"And you, my baby, are my strength. Never forget that. I love you."

He'd already told her that he loved her, and he'd been awake for less than an hour...Gloria had been right, then, in believing the two of them needed some alone time to sort out the issues they'd been having.

"Gloria," he said, reaching across the table for her hand, "I want to have another baby."

She took a deep breath. "I told you after the twins, I can't go through that again. It was so painful..."

Tears came to her eyes, remembering how badly she'd hurt after she'd given birth to two babies, one right after the other...she'd sometimes locked herself in the bathroom, sitting on the toilet for some relief from the insane amount of pressure, swelling and pain from her injuries.

Henry had known how badly she'd been hurting...she'd made him wait forever before they made love again, and she'd broken down sobbing in fear of the pain before he'd put his cock inside her...then she'd cried in pain when he'd impaled her.

It had felt like her first time with a lover all over again, only that time, her lover had a much larger cock.

"I know it hurt you, babygirl, but I know how happy babies make you."

"The twins are barely one year, Henry. Even *if* I were up to getting pregnant again, I want to focus on my babies' childhoods. I'd at least want to wait until they were in school."

Henry sighed. "Gloria, you're already thirty-four. We can't really afford to wait until the twins start school. You'll be too—"

"Oh, fuck," Gloria said, getting to her feet. "Don't you *dare* speak those words, or I might never let you fuck me again, much less get me pregnant."

He frowned. "I'm not saying anything about you getting old—"

"Well, that's fucking good," she said, "because you have a good decade on me."

"But men can be older when they have children. Women only have a certain window of time—"

"I know these things but thank you for reminding me."

"Babygirl, don't get upset. We were having a beautiful morning—"

"It's well after noon."

"I don't see the value in you being a bitch right now, Gloria."

"You hurt me."

He sighed, burying his face in his hands. "I always do. I can't say a word to you without hurting you.

"Forgive me for broaching the subject of more babies before it's too late, and you have to live with that regret for the rest of your life."

She brought her napkin to her mouth, doing her best to control her emotions...she didn't want to cry. She was afraid crying would make Henry angry, and that was the last thing that she needed.

Henry stood, coming to kneel beside her. He took her hands in his, making her look at him.

"Please don't cry. I didn't mean to hurt you."

"Is having more babies *really* that important to you?"

"I told you before we married that I wanted a big family."

She looked down at her feet. "I know, baby."

"I know you wanted children, too. Three might be enough for you. I at least want one more."

"Do you want the babies to just fall out, Henry? I thought you wanted to fuck a tight cunt."

"I can always fuck your ass," he joked.

She shook her head. "God, you're an asshole." She sighed. "It's a good thing I'm madly in love with you."

He wrapped his arms around her. "As am I, babygirl."

"I know...I know you are, baby. It's just that, sometimes..."

"Sometimes, what, Gloria?" Henry asked her...in a way that made her heart ache with love for him.

"I wonder why you've not asked me to sit in your lap so we can feed each other breakfast," Gloria said, smiling across the table at her husband.

"I know that if you got into my lap, you wouldn't end up eating anything. We'd be too busy fucking."

She smiled.

"Gloria...come over here."

She stood, easily and eagerly walking over to him, closing the distance between them.

He hadn't been wrong. The second her ass hit his lap, he grabbed tightly onto her butt cheeks, gripping her hard as he began making out with her, his tongue in her mouth, his pelvis griding up against her pussy as he thrust toward her, already rock hard for her.

Gloria could feel herself dripping into her panties, she was so horny. She already needed him to fuck her again; she supposed writing all morning had done it to her...that, or the way he was looking into her eyes as he thrust against her and held onto her.

He worked his mouth down her neck as he began removing her lingerie and slipped her silk robe off her shoulders, kissing down her arms as he moved his hands to her breasts.

He reached behind her to unsnap her bra, easing the straps down her shoulders, kissing his way down her neck as he tossed her bra aside, moving his mouth to her breast, above her nipple, as he began kissing her there.

Gloria buried her face in his hair, whimpering. She wasn't sure how much longer she could stand to take things slowly, although she also loved Henry for it.

She groaned as she reached down to unzip his trousers, eager to have his cock inside her, and he didn't stop her as he took her nipple into his mouth, sucking and biting her as she whimpered helplessly, tugging desperately at his trousers to get them down, to grant her access to his dick.

"Mmm, baby," he murmured against her breasts as she fondled his hard member.

"I need you inside me," she said.

"Anything for you, babygirl."

He shoved her thong to the side so the lacy scrap of fabric wouldn't get in the way of his cock impaling her. Reaching between her legs, he worked a finger between her folds as he felt how wet she was for him. "Oh, damn, baby."

"Mmm, I need you," she whimpered.

"I'm yours."

She took his cock between both of her hands, stroking him even harder, looking into his eyes as she touched him.

"Enough teasing."

She smiled. "My thoughts too. I need this more than you do, I think."

With that, Gloria positioned herself on top of Henry, angling his cock and lifting herself, him pressing against her pussy lips in a most tantalizing way.

"You're soaking."

"Yes, Henry, I am. I'm so fucking wet for you."

She slowly sank herself onto his cock, moaning loudly as he pressed deep inside her. She closed her eyes as she took him in, inch by inch, until all seven inches were wedged deep.

She pressed her forehead against his, panting as she held herself there, clenching her pussy around him, pulsing, making him moan.

"I don't know how you learned to do that, babygirl, but *fuck,* you're amazing."

"Mmm," she mumbled, pressing her mouth against his before she asked, "So I presume I'm better than your ex?"

"Am I better than yours, babygirl?" he countered.

"Bryson couldn't give me an orgasm. I had to get off later by myself."

Henry grabbed her hips and held her still as he thrust upward, deep inside her. "Fuck, I always get you off, don't I?"

Gloria laughed. "Fuck me harder."

He began fucking her up, deep inside her, holding her tightly, pulling her forward so he could suck on her nipples as he fucked her.

Gloria began riding him, meeting his thrusts, moaning loudly as their bodies slapped together, over and over. She kept moaning and whimpering as they fucked, feeling his cock hitting her cervix.

She started to grind against him...every time his head brushed against her g spot, she craved more...she whimpered louder as she got closer to orgasm, clenching her pussy tight, heightening her own pleasure as well as his.

"Yes, fuck! Keep doing that, babygirl," he said, driving higher and deeper inside her. "I love that fucking cunt, baby."

"I love your cock...*oh, fuck, Henry!"*

Gloria came incredibly hard, practically convulsing on Henry's lap as her orgasm ripped through her violently. She buried her face against his neck to muffle her screams, but he pulled her back by her hair as he said, "You don't have to be quiet. We're all alone."

He reached between their joined bodies then, and he rubbed her clit in hard circles, bringing her to her second orgasm while she was still coming down from her first, with him cumming deep inside her.

Gloria's body had more than it could take, as she shook.

Henry held her close, gently stroking her back as she came down from her orgasm. "Good girl. You're so good. I love you, Gloria."

She buried her face against his neck, working her fingers through his hair as she said, "I love you, baby."

He held her asscheeks as she came back down, then once she was calmed down and her orgasm had ended, he motioned for her to climb off his lap as he stood, taking her hands in his as he looked at her lovingly. “God, I’m glad you’re all mine.”

“I sure as fuck am.”

Gloria deliberately chose to ignore the fact that he’d ended their argument—over something legitimately serious—by fucking her and telling her how much he loved her; she was so desperate for his affection, she willingly overlooked it.

He walked her over to the full-length mirror in their dining room, beside the china cabinet, between the cabinet and the window.

She was nude, save her thong, which was still pushed to the side, Henry’s cum dripping out of her pussy as he stood behind her, gently cupping one breast in his hand as he kissed her shoulder.

Gloria gasped as she saw the enormous, black bruises down one side of her body...she must have hit the marble floor a lot harder than she’d realized.

“Oh my god, I look awful,” Gloria said, staring at her reflection in disbelief.

"Does it hurt?" Henry shook his head. "That was a stupid question. Of course, it hurts."

"I didn’t notice it until you showed me," Gloria said. "I was sore, but...goddamn."

"I guess no more fucking on the dining room table, yes?"

She shrugged. "It’s not so bad."

Henry laughed. "Sure, darling. You look like you've been hit by a truck."

She sighed, tired of looking at her injuries. She turned away from the mirror, facing her husband. She looked up at him, meeting his eyes as she felt his hands smoothing down her body, across her skin, as he reached down to cup her butt.

She reached up to kiss him.

He moved his mouth to her neck, nipping her lightly. "I want to spend the whole day buried deep inside your sweet cunt."

Gloria whimpered as he moved his fingers between her legs, feeling her wetness...she was ready for him again.

"Bedroom," he moaned against her neck, working his mouth down to her breasts, licking and sucking her soft flesh, then her nipples, making her arch her back hard, pressing her tits into his mouth.

"Henry," she moaned.

He lifted her, and Gloria wrapped her legs around his waist as he carried her to the bedroom, kissing her all the while.

Once reaching the bedroom, he laid her back across the bed, staring down at her for a few moments before he climbed on top of her.

He kissed her mouth, then he grabbed her hips and flipped her over onto her belly, being careful not to hurt her, as he turned her on the side that wasn't black with bruises.

He stroked her backside, up to where her shoulder blades protruded through her bony back, down to her soft, supple asscheeks.

"Your body is so perfect," he whispered, leaning forward and pressing his face between her cheeks.

Gloria whimpered, then moaned—loudly—as he began eating her ass.

"When I'm done with you, your pussy will be so sore you won't be able to walk."

He ended up fucking her from behind, holding her by her wrists over her head as she laid on her stomach and he thrust into her. He held both wrists in one hand, fingering her asshole as he fucked her hard, each deep thrust driving into her g spot, teasing her, as he wasn't ready to allow her to cum yet.

Gloria cried out as he shoved two fingers inside her asshole.

"Are you okay?" Henry asked.

"Yes," she panted. "Keep going."

He began fucking her harder, hammering into her sweet, wet pussy.

He pulled his fingers apart in a scissoring motion inside her ass, stretching her as his cock impaled her, making her cries even louder.

"Still?" he asked, almost breathlessly.

"Mmm, it hurts."

He kissed the back of her neck, dropping her wrists as he grabbed her hair in one hand so that he could kiss her, "Do you want me to stop?"

"No, just be gentler."

"With your ass?"

"Fuck me more gently," she whispered.

"Okay."

His thrusts slowed, but somehow, that wasn't what Gloria had wanted, either. She shifted her body against his, pushing back, asking for more.

"What do you want, Gloria?"

"Get behind me?"

He rolled her onto her side that wasn't bruised, positioning himself behind her as he thrust deep inside, holding onto one hand as he twisted the fingers of his other hand through her hair, pulling her head back against his chest so he had access to her lips and her neck, making out with her as he made slow love to her.

Gloria thrusted back, her movements gentle as she wiggled her ass against him.

"Mmm, baby, keep doing that," he said, grabbing one fleshy asscheek in his hand as he pulled her back against him, keeping his thrusts slow and deep.

She grabbed the sheets hard. "Mmm, yes, so fucking good, baby." She looked over her shoulder at him. "I love you."

"Babygirl, I love you." He wrapped one hand around her neck, drawing her in close to him, to kiss her deeply.

The sex was slow, and the orgasms intense and rolling; both Henry and Gloria were completely spent by the end of their lovemaking session, and they fell asleep together soon after.

It had been so long since Gloria had slept in Henry's arms after making love...it was her absolute favorite feeling in the world, being exhausted and entirely sexually sated as she slept in her husband's strong arms, against his hard chest.

She was happier than she'd been in ages, as she drifted off to sleep.

Gloria awakened later that evening, with the sunset muted light illuminating the bedroom.

She smiled, moaning as she stretched, reaching out beside her for Henry...finding the bed empty.

She sat up, glancing around the bedroom. "Henry?"

She got up out of bed, wincing at the soreness deep inside her...he'd fucked her harder than she realized. Even her asshole was sore from where he'd fingered her.

She went into the bathroom, but Henry wasn't there, either...perhaps he'd decided he wanted to fix them dinner?

She frowned, seeing her body in the mirror...she now had small bruises all over her breasts. She turned around, looking over her shoulder...sure enough, Henry had bruised her other hip and ass as well, but those bruises weren't hideous like the one covering the left side of her body.

She pulled on her robe and some thick wool socks, then she wandered into the rest of the house in search of Henry.

As a matter of fact, she did *not* find her husband...but she did find a note he'd left her..

Baby, I went to the pub. Be home late, don't wait up for me. I love you.

Henry

Gloria was deeply hurt. After the intimacy they had shared together, he was still going to go out to the pub...even though Gloria's mother had come all the way to London to watch their children so she and Henry could spend some time together privately.

She didn't understand how—after everything had happened between them—he could have simply decided to go off to the pub as though it were any other night.

As if the two of them hadn't turned a corner in their relationship; what else was she going to have to do in order to fix things between them?

She was tempted to start crying. She knew better than to call him, certain it would make him angry if she did...that he would find a way to turn it around on her, to make it seem as though she didn't trust him, that she was checking up on him.

Instead, she decided to clean up the kitchen, which turned into her cleaning the whole house and doing another load of laundry. She knew she needed to go check on her poor mother, wrangling the three babies all on her own, but at the same time Gloria was distraught, and she didn't want to upset her children if her mood was off.

And she sure as hell didn't want her mother to know that things were anything less than perfect between her and Henry. Mrs. Alexander already had her suspicions, Gloria knew.

Instead, she buried herself in getting her house clean and—for the first time in ages—got head on her laundry... which had only been possible because the babies weren't at home.

When Gloria's mother returned them to her, however, Gloria knew that she would have a mountain of laundry to do.

Her main concern—of course—was her marriage.

She didn't want to have more babies, and it had nothing to do with her not loving her husband.

Despite the cup of tea she'd made herself, before she snuggled into bed, having taken a long, hot shower to soothe her aching muscles, Gloria couldn't sleep.

She knew that the gnawing at the back of her mind was what kept her awake; she needed Henry.

And he wasn't coming home.

The feeling deep in her gut reminded Gloria so much of how she'd felt after each of her lovers had left her. No matter what Henry had promised, she still feared he was going to leave.

She grabbed her phone, using every ounce of willpower she possessed to keep from calling or texting Henry. Instead, Gloria found herself doing even worse...picking her phone up to open her social media.

Clicking on the inbox icon...

And continuing that conversation from earlier, the one she had ended abruptly in order to go fuck her husband.

Gloria spent the rest of her evening talking to a married man.

6

Chapter Six

Gloria continued her friendship with Dean.

She also started—with the help of her mother—working seriously on her new book.

Most things were going better in Gloria's life. She was working, and she felt more rested. Suddenly though, things between her and Henry were more strained than ever before.

Gloria told herself Dean was trouble, but she'd thought the same of Henry when they first met.

It wasn't that she wanted to leave Henry in order to be with Dean...that would have been preposterous. After all, Henry was her husband, the father of her babies...babies Gloria's mother was still helping to care for, as Henry was about as helpful as the flu.

Despite everything, Gloria was still in love with Henry. She longed to repeat their sex life from when Gloria's mother had first come to visit, and he had made love to her, held her, made out with her...when he had treated her as his wife, not as a sex toy.

It wasn't due to Gloria's lack of trying. She had done everything in her power to get Henry to stay home at night, and to be sweet and loving toward her again...

When he'd become distant as ever, she had turned to another man.

Dean.

Their relationship hadn't turned sexual yet, but it had become romantic in nature.

Gloria knew she was in too deep with him...and she could tell she wasn't going to be able to extricate herself from him. He wasn't going to let go without a fight.

Gloria woke early to write...Dean would always message her when he woke, first thing...even before he spoke to his girlfriend. Gloria was halfway through her novel, and if she kept up her momentum, it would be ready to be sent to her editor by Valentine's Day.

Gloria ignored Dean's texts until she'd completed Chapter Eleven of her book; that was the goal she had set for herself that day, and she was determined not to stop until she'd reached her goal.

It was noon when she finally stopped writing. Truth be told, she wanted to go wake Henry up, to talk to him...it was almost Christmas, and they *needed* to get some Christmas shopping done.

Also...the nonstop texts from Dean were beginning to get to her. He was far too demanding, especially since they hadn't even made their "relationship" in any way official, hadn't defined what they were...certainly hadn't made any plans to meet in person.

She finally picked up her phone to check her messages.

Good morning, babe. How are you today?
You must still be asleep. Hope you're doing well. I miss you.
Please text me, Gloria, I'm getting worried.
Gloria, text me.

And more similar texts, beginning at eight that morning, so for four hours, at least every fifteen minutes, never ceasing.

And it pissed Gloria off.

She was tempted not to text him back at all. It was what he deserved, being demanding of her and her time, of getting in the way of Gloria's writing...which, in her opinion, was unforgivable.

Yeah, I'm fine, Dean.
Why are you texting me so much? I've been writing.

She wanted to say more, but decided to leave it at that as she grabbed her cold tea and took a sip...she wanted more hot tea—she needed the caffeine—but she also knew she needed to sort things out with Dean before she went to Henry.

She only had to wait a few seconds before he responded...of course.

I was worried, you always text me in the morning. I'm sorry for annoying you.

Gloria sighed...that seemed normal for him. He had this way of getting defensive, Gloria had noticed, and he'd done it the first time when she'd been concerned about the two of them getting too close, manipulating her, plain and simple...

But truth be told, Gloria had been conditioned to manipulation by Henry himself, so she'd felt guilty for hurting Dean, and had been unable to cut him off...as she should have done, in order to protect her marriage. She'd wanted that marriage to Henry more than anything, and she should have been more than willing to sacrifice everything for it.

Alright, now I'm going to spend some time with my husband. Do you have a problem with that?

She knew that she was being a brat to him...and she suspected that Dean could see right through her.

He knew how close he was to having Gloria wrapped around his finger. To be fair, it didn't take much.

I do. He doesn't deserve you.

And you think that I would be better off with you, don't you?

Yes, Gloria, I do.

She closed her eyes... damn.

She thought that she was the one in control, and with one statement, Dean snatched her power away from her.

Gloria?

I'm married.

And I've got a girlfriend.

Gloria had a lot more to lose than Dean. She was married with three babies. She loved Henry.

But it was impossible for her to deny anymore that she was falling for Dean, too.

I have children.

Gloria, I don't want to pretend anymore.

Knowing that she couldn't deal with the emotional fallout of the admission of their feelings, Gloria locked her phone...in her haste, she knocked her laptop off the mahogany desk onto the marble floor; Gloria heard the telltale crack as the screen broke.

Before she even picked it up, she knew her laptop screen was broken.

Again.

She sighed. It was all Dean's fault...his fault she was beyond stressed, that she was struggling with her relationship with Henry, and his fault she could barely focus on the one constant in her life: writing.

She immediately got on her phone and—since her laptop was too broken to use—searched up the laptop repair place...as much as it spiked Gloria's anxiety, she really had no choice but to call and make an appointment to have her laptop repaired.

She couldn't write a book without it.

After about half an hour, Gloria had finally gotten through to a repair specialist. She had begged for him to agree to fix her laptop that very day...he refused. Gloria couldn't help thinking that he hadn't liked that she was an American.

Finally—after Gloria promised an extra £500 to have her laptop placed at the front of the line—he agreed...but told Gloria that she had to have the laptop at the shop by 3:00 PM that day, and he would have it ready for her by noon the day after Christmas.

The problem was, Gloria didn't leave the penthouse. She even had groceries delivered.

However, Gloria had promised Briella—Henry's oldest with his ex—she would go Christmas shopping with her.

Terrified as Gloria was about going out, she didn't want to disappoint Briella...she liked Briella just fine, and the young woman was only ten years her junior, despite being her husband's daughter.

She didn't want to seem weak to Briella. She didn't want Henry's daughter to realize just how unwell her father's second wife was, how unstable the mother of her half siblings was.

Gloria had a shower and got ready, but she first went to the kitchen. It was spotless since the babies were still with Mrs. Alexander, but that would change that evening, as Charlotte, Henry's youngest daughter, and Brett, the baby of the family, his son, were having Christmas with their father and half-sisters.

That was another reason Gloria had been so stressed. She'd been cooking and cleaning for days in preparation for the holiday, and she put up decorations the day before. She'd been cooking all morning, and the Christmas tree was to be delivered around six that evening.

Their plan was to have dinner, decorate the tree, then bake homemade cookies. Once the cooking was done, they would put the babies to bed, then would have a slightly more grown-up party, in which they would watch a Christmas film—*Love, Actually* (which Gloria despised)—and would have dessert and some wine and spirits before bed.

The following morning, they would open gifts and have breakfast, then early afternoon, Henry's children would leave.

Gloria—while she was looking forward to spending the holidays with her stepchildren—was exhausted, thinking about all she had to do in the next fifty or so hours.

Gloria was in the middle of mixing her sweet potatoes in the food processor when Henry finally emerged from the bedroom...the only thing he'd done, which had been a request of hers, once her mother came to stay and help out for a bit, was to get into bed with her once he finally rolled in from the pub...no matter how late.

He came up behind her, wrapping his arms around her waist. "You look wonderful, darling," he said, kissing her neck.

"Thank you." She'd spent more time getting ready for her shopping excursion with Briella than she had getting ready for the last date that Henry had taken her on, which had been back when she'd been pregnant with Eva.

It had been over three years since he'd taken his wife on a date and realizing that fact anew broke her a bit.

Henry felt her tense in his embrace. "Are you okay?" he asked.

She nodded. "Just nervous."

"About?"

She turned to meet his eyes. "Shopping."

"Most women love to shop."

She finally had the sweet potatoes mixed; she had to put them in the pan to stick into the oven. She planned to cover half of the casserole with her nut garnish and the other with marshmallows. Henry's children liked the nut garnish, and Gloria preferred the marshmallows, as did her own biological children. She supposed she had the tastes of a small child, but that didn't bother her.

She knew she was a mess.

"I do love shopping," she said, beginning to top her casserole, "but you know...I get nervous to leave the house."

"I know, babygirl, but you're going to be fine," he said, taking her face in his hands and turning her to kiss him.

"I hope so...I don't want to act like an idiot in front of your family."

"My children love you, Gloria. My son adores you. I think he's jealous of me that I found you first."

Gloria rolled her eyes. "Right."

"And Briella thinks you're her age. I'm surprised she's not asked you to go clubbing."

Gloria laughed.

"Are you going to be okay, baby?" he asked, gently kissing her lips.

She nodded. "I...I've got a favor to ask of you, though."

"Sure, darling. What do you need?" he asked, wrapping his arms tightly around her and holding her close, making her feel safe.

"Thank you," she whispered.

"Anything for you, my darling."

He'd become more affectionate toward her recently. Gloria figured it was due to them spending more time together. She certainly loved how sweet and attentive he had been toward her. They had sex at least every other day. Sometimes, they played BDSM style...other times, they made love.

"Do you miss it?"

"Miss what, baby?" she asked, looking up into his eyes.

"Us."

"I thought that we'd been doing well lately?" Gloria asked, confused.

"Yes, we have. I meant the way that things were before we had children."

She slightly pulled back, looking at him.

He trailed his fingers down her cheeks. "I don't mean anything negative by that, babygirl. I love our children more than anything. I only meant, we used to have so much more time for the two of us, you know?

"Of course," she said, curling into him. "But we have time now, with my mother here."

"After the children go home tomorrow...why don't the two of us spend some time together? I want to take you out on a date, make you feel like the most valuable woman alive." He took her hand in his, kissing her fingers. "Because you are, Gloria...when it comes to me."

She smiled. "I miss it, too. Being shown off by you."

Henry moaned, kissing her neck hard. "Oh, babygirl, you have no idea how much I love that. You're *mine,*" he emphasized, turning her on.

She wished she had more time before she had to leave...she needed him. She wanted to feel him inside her, stretching her, filling her up.

He felt the same way, she could tell, as he fondled her breasts through the shirt she was wearing. He gave her right breast a tight squeeze as he said, "I can't wait to fuck you tonight, baby."

She moaned. "It's going to be a long day, waiting for that to happen." She smiled, turning in his arms to face him, looking up into his face. "I love you."

He leaned in over her, kissing her long and hard as he said, "I love you too, babygirl."

She sighed, picking up the casserole dish. "I'm going to stick this in the refrigerator. Everything is done, ready to be put in the oven or on the stove this evening. I've got to have the turkey in before Briella and I are to be back this afternoon..."

My son will be here. He can stick it in, just write down instructions. You might also call and remind him."

Gloria nodded. "Okay."

"What was that favor?" he asked. "Rearrange your guts?"

Gloria laughed, feeling her face get hot before she said, "Well, that...but I also wanted you to take my laptop to the tech store to get it worked on. I must have it there by two this afternoon, and I didn't want to make Brielle go with me to drop it off..."

Henry frowned. "What happened to your laptop, babygirl?"

She sighed. "It's stupid. I just knocked it off my desk...and you know what a marble floor does to technology."

"Yes, I've had to replace a lot of screens before I got a protective case for my phone."

She nodded. "Right."

Gloria had the feeling that Henry could tell there was something she wasn't saying about how her laptop had gotten broken...of course, he had no idea about Dean.

"My pin is 4723," Gloria said, reaching up to gently brush her lips against his. "So you can log on and make sure everything is in working order—save the screen, of course—before you bring it home."

"Okay." He kissed her forehead softly, then said, "I love you, Gloria. I'm so lucky you're mine." He pulled her in closer. "I know things haven't been easy lately, but I promise you, baby...I'm going to start treating you better."

"I'm more than happy with you," she whispered, hugging him tightly.

She wondered why she'd entertained the possibility of an affair with Dean, when she'd fought so hard for her relationship with Henry, when she'd given him three children...when he was her everything and meant the whole world to her.

"Good," Henry said, hugging her tightly. "Because I have no idea what I'd do without you, and I truly mean that, Gloria. You've become my whole life."

Gloria knew what he said wasn't true...no matter how desperately she'd needed to hear those words, or how greatly she longed for them to *be* true.

If Gloria was truly his whole world, then why on earth would he have needed the pub?

But she wasn't about to ask that question. Instead, Gloria wrapped her arms tightly around him. "I love the sound of that." She reached up, pressing her lips against his neck, then she whispered into his ear, "I'll give you anything you want tonight, Henry. I'll let you do whatever you want to do to me. Okay, baby?"

"Even your ass?"

"Anything," she said, knowing she was horny enough to be down for whatever rough and dirty sex he had in mind for the two of them.

It disturbed Gloria to think she'd almost let her guard down and crossed the line with Dean, risking her marriage to Henry for him.

Henry kissed her, then the doorbell rang, announcing the arrival of Henry's eldest.

Gloria took a deep breath. "I love Briella dearly. I hope you don't think that my nerves have anything to do with her, because I'm thrilled to be spending the day with her. I love our holiday shopping tradition...but I believe that's the last time I went to the shops, a year ago."

"Babygirl," Henry said, taking her by her elbows and gently drawing her in to him, "when is the last time that you left the house?"

She swallowed. "When we took the girls down to greet my mother, when she first arrived here."

"When is the last time that you went out of the actual building, Gloria? When you were outdoors?"

"On the balcony—"

"Totally outside the house."

"Last summer. When we took the girls to the zoo."

Henry closed his eyes, sighing. "I guess I hadn't noticed. Baby...you need help."

"I'm fine, I just don't like going outside." She shook her head. "I've been writing, I'm cooking, cleaning, raising a family—"

"Don't get defensive," he said, immediately going into his dominant mode.

"I'm sorry."

"Honesty, not excuses. I'm not angry with you, Gloria. I'm concerned." He frowned. "Do you really think that you can handle today?"

"Yes, I can," I said, heading down the hallway and to the door as the doorbell rang a second time. "I will *not* let Briella down, nor will I ruin our holiday traditions, Henry."

He wrapped his arm around her waist, holding her steady as he whispered into her ear, "I know, baby. But I can't have you hurting yourself or getting worse."

She turned, pressing her head into his chest as she hugged him. "I won't. I promise, baby."

With that, Gloria was all smiles as she swung open the door and greeted Briella. "Hi, sweetheart, it's so good to see you!"

Briella hugged her, then her father. "I've missed you both so much!"

"Blackpool isn't so far away," Henry reminded her. "You can always come visit."

"I'm so busy working, Dad," she said. "But I do miss you."

He kissed her forehead. "How's the waitressing?"

Briella had gone to college to act. She *was* an actress, but she mostly supported herself—in the meantime, she always said—by serving at a restaurant in her home city.

"You still living with that fucker?" Henry asked.

Briella sighed, and Gloria said, "Let her into the house before you start grilling her about her personal life...which isn't any of your business."

"Thank you, Gloria," Briella said, handing her coat and handbag to her father, as she followed Gloria into the living room.

"Do you need anything? Some water, or a drink?"

"No, we have reservations for lunch at Studio Frantzén in Harrods," Briella said. "I'm saving my appetite for that."

"Good idea. And for dinner, too," Gloria said, smiling. "I spent the whole week preparing for tonight. We're making cookies later with the little ones."

"Sounds amazing. Where are they, by the way?"

Gloria took a breath. "My mother came to stay for a while...she's been caring for them. Your father and I..."

Briella smiled, reaching over to place her hand against Gloria's arm. "No need to say anything. I can't imagine how you manage to fuck with three small children."

Gloria felt her face get hot.

"Oh, don't be a prude, I know my father." Briella rolled her eyes.

Gloria knew Briella had a blasé attitude toward sex—even when it concerned her own father and her step-mother—but it still took some getting used to.

"We should get going," Briella said, tossing her long red hair over her shoulder. "Come."

Gloria headed out of the penthouse, following her stepdaughter...her heart was hammering in her chest, her palms sweating.

Henry was standing in the kitchen. "You ladies on your way out?"

"Yes," Briella said, putting her coat on.

Henry wrapped his arm around Gloria's waist, drawing her close. "I love you, babygirl." He lowered his voice as he said, "If you need me, call me. You can do this."

He took her face in his hands, looking into her eyes as he said, "I know you can do this. You're going to be fine, babygirl. I love you so much."

Then Henry kissed her, and she forgot everything else, her anxiety, her fear over leaving the house...even Dean, her little secret who had nearly ruined her life.

But it was Christmas, things were going well between her and Henry, and she was going to focus on her family. It was their Christmas together, after all.

She didn't have room for Dean, not then, not ever.

She kissed Henry once more, then she grabbed her own coat. Henry helped her into it, wrapping it around her, kissing the back of her neck before he smoothed her curly blond hair down.

"I love you," she said again, kissing her husband goodbye.

"I love you, darling. I'll see you tonight. Don't forget, call or text Brett about the turkey."

She smiled. "Bye, baby."

She and Briella finally got onto the elevator and headed down to the parking garage, where Gloria's Land Rover was parked. Henry drove it regularly, but Gloria herself hadn't driven since she'd been about four months with Eva. She had no idea how she was going to manage to drive after three years, but the more that she thought about it, she knew, the harder it was going to be.

"Gloria?"

She glanced over at her stepdaughter. "I'm sorry, what was that?"

"Are you okay?"

Gloria forced herself to smile. "Perfect, why?"

Briella smiled. "Are you going to unlock the car?"

She reached into her pocket, pulling out the key fob and clicking the doors unlocked. Briella tossed her handbag into the floorboards, buckling in her seat.

You can do this, Gloria told herself. *You drove all over Atlanta and Los Angeles...you can drive anywhere.*

She got into the driver's side, starting the car and backing out of her parking spot; her heart was hammering in her chest, and she was about to throw up, but outwardly she displayed a calm demeanor.

She was protecting Briella from knowing her stepmother was a helpless, pathetic woman afraid of driving her car, not to mention afraid of walking outside her own home.

"Have you ever eaten there?"

"Pardon?" Gloria asked.

She needed to focus.

"Are you okay?"

Gloria smiled. "I think I just have mother brain."

"I've heard of that," Briella said. "Sounds terrible."

Gloria laughed, grateful for the distraction of conversation as she pulled onto the busy street. "I'm guessing you don't want babies anytime soon?"

"I don't think Ben is ever going to ask me to marry him," Briella said. "Why would he, when he's getting the milk for free?"

Gloria wasn't getting into that. She had listened to Henry go on in fury when Vic had allowed Briella to move in with her boyfriend. She'd known better than to try to give him advice when it came to his children with Vic...she loved them, but they weren't hers to have any say in how they were raised, especially since they were nearly grown, anyway.

She knew Henry still held a grudge against Vic for allowing Briella to leave home and to get a flat with "that boy..." but at the same time, Briella had been dating Ben since she was seventeen, and Gloria could tell they were in love.

She was with Vic, secretly. Gloria knew if she'd met Henry when she was seventeen, she would have moved in with him in a heartbeat...long before she was out of college, as Briella had done.

"He will," Gloria said. "If you decide that you want to get married."

"Would you not recommend it?"

"Oh, I'm very happy with your father," Gloria said.

"I can tell. Three babies in less than four years."

Gloria smiled.

"I know he's not an easy man."

Gloria swallowed...she wasn't sure it was an appropriate conversation for her to have with her stepdaughter.

"It's okay. You don't think I haven't heard it from my mother all these years?"

Gloria didn't answer. "You know as well as I do that all couples have their issues."

"But I know how he can be."

At least the stressful conversation was preventing Gloria from focusing on how stressed she was over driving.

"He's wonderful."

"Right," Brielle said.

Gloria drove as calmly as possible, going over and over in her mind how she loved Henry, she loved his family, and she was happy with her life.

She needed no convincing of those facts.

"Have you ever eaten here?"

"No," Gloria said. "You?"

Briella laughed. "No, babes. I'm a waitress."

Gloria figured Briella had wanted to eat at an exclusive restaurant and knew that the only way she could afford it was through her rich stepmother. Gloria didn't mind. Her love language *was* gift-giving, after all.

"Are you ready for Christmas?"

"Yes. It's so fun with babies, but at the same time, you have such high expectations to meet."

"I loved the Christmas card you sent to me and Ben. Eva is such a cutie...she could have been my full sister, for her red hair."

Gloria swallowed...no, no. Eva was *hers*...her baby with Henry, and there was no debate. She knew Briella meant no harm by what she'd said, hadn't meant to imply anything.

Gloria parked the Land Rover. "You ready?"

Briella reached over and grabbed Gloria's arm, gently. "Sweets, I realize what I said was insensitive."

Was Gloria that bad at hiding her feelings, she wondered? "No, of course not, everything is fine."

"I know how much you love my Dad," Briella said, as the two ladies headed for the elevator. "I know that it's hard for you, knowing he has another family."

"I love you and your brother and sister. And I have a lot of respect for your mother."

"I know...but I think a lot about how I would feel if things were to go south between me and Ben, and if I married an older man who had been married and had children with another woman...I don't think I could do it."

"You and Ben will get married...it's not something that you need to worry about, sweetheart," Gloria said.

"I don't...I just try to put myself in your shoes."

"I'm happy," Gloria said. "I'm very lucky. Your father...he's the love of my life."

The women made it to the restaurant. Gloria could tell Briella was preening over the thrill of being a patron at such an exclusive restaurant, even if it was early in the day, not quite so luxurious as it would have been in the evening.

Gloria could afford the meal. She loved her biological children more than her stepchildren, and Gloria always felt a bit guilty about that, which was why she never said "no" to anything they asked her for, be it expensive, extravagant gifts *or* lunches at upscale restaurants at Harrods.

"What are you ordering?" Briella asked, once the women were sitting at their table. It *was* one of the best tables in the restaurant, and they were certainly on display...of course, the people there to see them at that hour of the afternoon weren't those whom Briella was hoping to impress.

"I guess I always had this fantasy that I would be discovered," Briella said, laughing as though she were embarrassed.

"It would make breaking into an impossible industry easier and would progress your career much faster."

Briella smiled. "I'm so glad that at least *you* believe this life is a possibility for me," she said. "My mother sure doesn't. I think she regrets allowing me to study drama in college."

"Your father believes in your dreams," Gloria offered.

Briella smiled. "Well, you and I both know that he's not the most connected with reality."

Gloria wondered what Briella *really* thought about her father...to be fair, though, Henry hadn't been around much. Gloria supposed he'd spent as much time at the pub as he had at home back then, too; that, and he was more into talking about how he loved being a father and having tons of children than he was in actually showing up for them. Even Gloria could admit that.

After all, it was the reason her own poor mother was spending the Holiday season in London, caring for her daughter's three children, rather than back in Atlanta running all her own social events.

In fact, Gloria knew her father was upset with her mother for being in London, for missing the social season, for not hosting all of the swanky holiday parties where he pretended he still had a political career...one which hadn't been ruined by his brother's scandals.

It was all about appearances for Gloria's father...always *had* been.

All the more reason why—Gloria supposed—he'd tried to silence her *and* her mother over what his brother had done to her...to Gloria, from the age of fourteen, up until she'd graduated high school and finally felt like she was free to speak her mind, since she'd no longer have to live under the same roof as the man who had refused to allow her to speak out...the man who hadn't kept his own daughter safe.

It had been a scandal. It had ruined her father's political career...and truthfully, Gloria's proudest accomplishment hadn't been graduating college with her English degree and honors...hadn't been marrying Bryson, for certain, but not even marrying her true love, Henry. Her brightest moment of success wasn't even the birth of one or all of her daughters.

No.

Gloria's greatest accomplishment of all time had been the day she came home with her high school diploma, had a massive grad party with all of her father's powerful friends in attendance—her disgusting uncle included—and she had looked right into his eyes, as she had given the greatest public speech of her life, in which she recounted the details of all her uncle had done to her for the past four years...in great detail.

She had spared nothing, from the pain, fear, and humiliation of her first time being taken from her by brutal force, to every single time that he had touched her, used her, and molested her.

She'd spoken those words in front of a huge crowd, full of the most powerful people in the country...and she'd not shed a tear.

She'd spent four years crying over the pain he'd caused her, and her little speech was her moment of strength, not of weakness or fear.

He'd been arrested that very night, and he was still in jail, as far as Gloria knew.

Not that she kept up with him.

"Gloria?"

Gloria brought herself back to the present, focusing on her stepdaughter as she sat across the table from her. They had their drinks, but Gloria was sitting still, staring across the room.

Briella was watching her, concerned. "Are you okay?"

Gloria nodded. "Of course. Sorry, just dipped out for a bit."

"I could tell...it's okay. I'm just a little worried because it seems as though you've done that a lot today, already."

Henry never mentioned her past. Of course, she'd told Javier, and he'd confessed his own sexual trauma to her, and Bryson had done his research about it, even found a video online of Gloria giving her graduation speech, and he'd confronted her about it...which had very nearly destroyed their relationship, as Gloria felt it was none of his business to be researching her rape and trauma in order to converse with her about it.

"This time of year brings up a lot of memories from my past...and I'm forced to think about my family. If you want to call them that."

Briella frowned. "That sounds terrible."

"I'm not going to burden you with my past."

Briella lowered her gaze to the table. "I um...I think that I know what you're talking about."

Gloria sighed...of *course* her stepchildren had probably researched her and knew all about her and what her uncle had done to her.

"How long have you known?" Gloria asked.

"Oh...not long after you and Dad were married. Actually...one of my friends mentioned it, so I had to look it up for myself...I'm sorry, Gloria."

"Don't be sorry. It's understandable that you'd want to know what happened...just, I mean...silence was my shackles. Me speaking out, that was me breaking those shackles and freeing myself."

"Are you okay now?"

"I mean...I suppose. I'm married and have my own family now...all things that he was unable to take away from me. Despite how he tried to."

"I'm so sorry."

Gloria sighed. "Don't be sorry. That's what I tell everyone. Feeling sorry for me for something that was done to me as a teenager isn't going to help anyone. Just be diligent...protect those at risk and believe survivors." Gloria forced a smile. "That's all I ask."

"And it's why you write your books."

"Partially."

Briella nodded. "Gloria...you're kind of my hero, you know."

Her love for her sweet—albeit misguided and a bit airheaded—stepdaughter grew in that moment, more than she'd thought possible.

"I admire you, Briella, for being a brave, kind woman. I'm proud of you for sticking with both your drama degree and with serving. I know how hard you work, and for a job you don't even want.

"Things are going to get better."

What Gloria *didn't* tell her stepdaughter was that, while things might get *better*, that didn't always mean that she would get exactly what she wanted.

Briella might surprise her, but Gloria suspected that she would follow the same footsteps as her mother. She already had half a decade on Vic when it came to having babies, as Vic was twenty when Briella had been born, and Henry was twenty-one.

Gloria still suspected Briella would end up marrying Ben because she got pregnant, and they'd have several children together. Briella would probably always be a server, and her acting career would never amount to anything.

But Briella would be a good mother, and a homemaker, and she'd find happiness in her own way, because she did love Ben.

Gloria wasn't sure why she was sitting there thinking about her stepdaughter's future instead of enjoying a *very* expensive meal with her...she hadn't even decided what to order yet.

"What are *you* getting?" Gloria asked, glancing down at her menu.

The two ladies had their lunch, then they headed into the rest of the shopping center to get some Christmas shopping done.

"Where would you like to start?" Gloria asked, walking with Briella through the mall.

"Bulgari has a pop-up I want to check out," Briella said. "And Dior."

Of course...to be fair, Harrods didn't really have inexpensive shops like Zara...unlike the Beverly Center back in Los Angeles, where Gloria had gone back when she actually left her apartment and drove her car.

She wondered if having children was what had turned her into such a coward, although deep down, Gloria knew that she was very sick with anxiety.

At one point, Gloria and Briella were in the dressing rooms, trying on some dresses. Gloria knew she was going to have to attend the New Years' Eve party, as she did every year, and she hadn't bought a new evening gown in ages, so she decided that there was no better opportunity for it than in that moment, when she was out of her house and at the shops. She sure as hell wasn't planning on leaving her home again once she finally got back that evening.

"What do you think?"

Gloria had her own sapphire colored evening gown halfway on, when she turned to look at Briella, who looked stunning–beyond, actually–in her emerald-colored mermaid style gown. It looked more like a prom dress, but Briella was so pretty, and it made her amazing body look so good.

"I love it. You look perfect," Gloria said, smiling.

"So do you. Damn, Gloria, those babies made your tits amazing."

Gloria felt her face flush. "Um...thank you. I think."

"Don't be a prude. I know you're not. You couldn't be, and still be married to my father."

"I'm not a prude."

"Nah...what happened here?"

Briella stepped closer, her fingertips trailing lightly against the uppermost swell of Gloria's cleavage, where her skin was still slightly bruised from Henry's sucking them and kissing so hard.

Gloria turned away. "Can you zip this for me?"

Briella did as Gloria had asked. "I didn't mean to embarrass you."

"You didn't...I don't know, Briella, I guess I *am* a prude. My family never discussed sex openly. Not even..."

"After what happened to you."

Gloria hesitated, checking herself out in the mirror. "Um...what do you think?"

"You look amazing. My father will eat you alive."

Gloria nodded. "Then maybe I should look for something less provocative."

"Why, he doesn't want you showing off to other men or something?"

"I don't want to be a distraction," Gloria said, starting to unzip the dress again. "Can you help me?"

Briella helped her back out of the dress, but when it had slipped off, Briella gasped. "What the fuck?"

Gloria had almost forgotten about the huge bruises on her side from falling off the dining room table. "Your father didn't do this."

"I sure as fuck hope not."

"I fell."

Briella crossed her arms over her chest. "That's convincing."

"Okay...your father was eating me on the dining room table, and I came so hard that I fell off. Is that more believable?"

Briella laughed a little. "Yeah, it is."

Gloria nodded. "Your father would never hurt me."

"I know. I mean, logically...but I know what you just told me about believing victims."

"Your father has never put his hands on me."

Which wasn't completely true, considering he'd slapped her face. But, Gloria knew, he hadn't slapped her in order to hurt her.

"That's good."

"Yes. So, are you going to get that gorgeous dress?"

"Are you?" Briella asked.

Both ladies bought their dresses. They continued shopping...Gloria was surprised to notice her anxiety had lessened dramatically, which she hadn't expected, especially considering the conversation she'd had with Briella, and knowing that her stepdaughter knew about Gloria's kinky sexual relationship with Briella's own father.

Finally, it was late afternoon, and Gloria drove them home, her Land Rover's backseat piled with gifts...as well as the two dresses that the ladies had purchased, and shoes and handbags to wear with their dresses on New Years' Eve.

The only thing that had happened to throw a wrench into Gloria's wonderful day with her stepdaughter was when she'd had to call Brett to tell him to put the turkey in the oven, and she'd seen all of the missed calls and messenger notifications that Dean had been trying to get into contact with her. It had made Gloria feel sick, because he hadn't let up at all, all day, despite having said several times something to the effect of "I'm going to send one last message," which had turned into messaging her all damn day, like a man obsessed.

Which, unfortunately, she feared he was.

"Are you okay?" Briella asked, noticing Gloria's anxiety.

"Yeah, I just hope I didn't wait too long to ask your brother to put the turkey in."

She'd been lying...there was no way for her to tell her stepdaughter that she'd done something so wrong as speaking intimately to another man, only to end up cutting him off. Gloria was grateful Dean lived in another country, so that he couldn't actually hunt her down or show up at her house.

She wondered if she should tell Henry about him. She knew it would infuriate him, hearing of her having such a close relationship with another man.

She figured Dean was a secret she was going to have to carry with her until he faded until a mere close call from her past, as she worked toward developing a deeper, more loving and emotional relationship with her Henry.

Dean was insignificant.

She parked in her spot in the penthouse parking garage, then she called the concierge and asked them to carry in their packages.

She and Briella entered the penthouse...Charlotte and Brett greeted them. Gloria hugged both of her stepchildren, then thanked Brett for putting the turkey in the oven.

"Is your father home yet?" Gloria asked.

"No, he said it will be at least half past six," Charlotte said. "Can I help with dinner?"

Soon, with the help of her stepchildren, Gloria had Christmas dinner in the works, the smells of cooking food tantalizing.

She'd really wanted Henry there before she sent for her mother to bring the babies up. She didn't think she could manage getting dinner on the table *and* having her babies–especially her sweet Eva, whom she knew missed her terribly–underfoot...not without her husband there to help.

When six-thirty arrived and Henry still wasn't home, Gloria had no choice but to collect her mother and babies without him...asking her stepchildren to watch dinner while she went to get their half-siblings.

By the time Gloria reached her mother's flat, she was in tears, and her mother frowned, asking, "What has Henry done now?"

"He's late getting home," Gloria said, putting her face in her hands as she sobbed.

"Sweetheart, we don't have time for tears. It's Christmas dinner. You have his children *and* yours to deal with. You don't have time for your husband being his imbecile self."

Gloria shook her head. "I didn't think that he was going to let me down today, of all days."

"Well, he has, and he doesn't deserve your tears."

Gloria couldn't help thinking how she'd been completely let down by *both* men in her life...even the one who was only in her life peripherally.

"Are you sure that this is all there is to it?" Mrs. Alexander asked. "You're not crying over something else? Did he hurt you?"

"No. He's just let me down a lot."

"Well, that's nothing new then, is it? Come on. You chose to marry a man like Henry and to give him children...that means you're going to have to suck it up and deal with him."

Gloria knew her mother was right...and that her husband was an asshole.

"I guess I just thought that, since it's his only Christmas with his other children, he wouldn't want to miss it," Gloria said, shrugging like it didn't matter...although it broke her.

"Come, darling."

"I'm sure Eva can't wait to go home."

"She's very excited about making cookies...and about seeing her older brother and sisters."

Gloria had to smile. In fact, the only thing that *could* have made Gloria happy was spending time with her precious Eva...the little part of Henry that never hurt her, never let her down, and always brought her nothing but joy.

"Where is she?" Gloria asked.

There was no need to ask, however, as Eva ran from the back of the house into her mother's arms.

Gloria scooped Eva up in her arms. "I missed you so much, sweetheart. How have you and your Gramma been getting on?"

"We've had fun." Eva laid her head against her mother's shoulder. "I want to go home now."

Gloria laughed, kissing Eva's head. "And how are your sisters?"

"They're mean."

Gloria caught her mother's eye, and Mrs. Alexander simply shook her head. "They *are* kind of mean to Eva."

Gloria felt her brow furrow, as she wondered how on earth two babies could possibly be *mean* to their older sister. She knew the twins had their own secret language—as twins did—despite how young they were. She figured as they got older, Eva would feel excluded from their twin connection, so perhaps Henry wasn't so wrong in wanting to have more children.

But how much could Eva really connect with a sibling so much younger? Gloria had wanted to have her children one right after the other, so they would always have each other, would always have a friend.

Of course, Gloria had no qualms about Eva being her little bestie, but she knew for Eva's sake, she needed to have friends her own age. Gloria only hoped she would find that connection with her younger siblings. Not that Gloria wasn't happy to have the twins...they gave her so much joy, always being devious and making her laugh.

Maybe it would get better once Eva started school...she'd make some friends and she would be able to have someone who wasn't intrinsically connected with another human, excluding her from their little bubble, as the twins were already doing.

"So, you think we should start without him?" Gloria asked, shifting Eva to her uninjured hip, flinching at the pain of Eva's little boot kicking into the still sore flesh before she had moved her to her opposite side.

Gloria noticed her mother watching her closely, her brow furrowing as she watched her daughter flinching in pain.

Gloria shook her head. "It's nothing," she said, softly, so that only her mother could hear...she knew that Mrs. Alexander suspected abuse on Henry's part.

"Sure."

Gloria had more to worry about than what her mother thought was going on between her and Henry...like where the hell even *was* her husband, and why the fuck wasn't he home, when Gloria was slaving away to create a gorgeous holiday meal and experience for *his* own family?

She could have spent that time writing or spending time with her own babies...anything but getting the house ready and cooking for *days* for Henry's children, food that she and her own children didn't even eat.

She forced her angry thoughts aside, however, as she nodded at her mother. "Well, let's go, shall we?"

She could feel her mother's eyes on her all the way there, judging not her, but the situation, and surely Henry. After all, Gloria hadn't painted her husband in the best light anyway, being in tears over the fact he wasn't home when he was supposed to be, that the one thing he'd promised her, he'd failed her.

Mrs. Alexander carried one twin and the diaper bag in the other hand, while Gloria held Eva on her good hip and Cheye's carrier in her opposite hand, almost buckling under the weight, flinching each time the baby carrier hit her sore side.

The elevator opened into the penthouse, and Gloria put Eva down, as the little girl ran as hard and fast as she could into Charlotte's waiting arms.

"I missed you!" Charlotte cooed, kissing Eva's cheek as she hugged her. "You're getting so big!"

That was why she did it, Gloria told herself, as she watched the sweet interaction between her oldest daughter and her middle stepchild; she did it so all her children could be together and have somewhat of a relationship with each other, in spite of the oddness of the situation and the age differences.

Family was very important to Gloria, perhaps because her own flesh and blood had hurt her so badly and disowned her so easily.

"I put the turkey in just like you said."

"Thank you, Brett," Gloria said, checking the turkey, which was ready to come out, but Henry wasn't home yet.

She refused to let her perfect Christmas dinner be ruined simply because her husband couldn't seem to get his ass away from the pub.

"Can I do anything else to help?"

Henry's youngest with Vic—and his only son—was now sixteen, and nearly old enough to be considered an adult. He was a kind, gentlemanly young man. Gloria sometimes wondered where he'd learned that behavior from, considering the paternal role model he'd had throughout his life.

"No, thank you," Gloria said. "You really saved me, Brett. I don't know what I would have done without you."

She could tell he was feeling proud of himself, and that made Gloria smile. She turned her back away from him so he wouldn't see her amusement or become embarrassed. Gloria knew Brett had a bit of a crush on her. It was weird, but he was a sweet young man, so she didn't mind.

The turkey looked fine, so Gloria turned the oven down on warm. The things on the stove were warming as well. She had the rolls warming; they were only waiting on Henry to arrive.

She was trying her best not to allow her anger to get the better of her, but Gloria was heartbroken.

She was fighting with everything inside her not to cry, but when Briella came in to check on the food and to see if there was anything that she could do, she saw the tears in Gloria's eyes and the frustration written across her face.

Briella placed her hands on Gloria's shoulders. "Are you okay, babes?"

Gloria wasn't about to badmouth her husband to his daughter, so she swallowed. "I just don't know where your father is."

"Gloria...I know as well as anyone how he is. Is there any chance...or, I mean, do you know...is he..."

Gloria shook her head vehemently. "Of course not."

"Okay."

"I think the stress of having three small children has gotten to him more than he wants to admit to. And getting out of the house is his only respite."

"And what's your respite, Gloria?" Briella asked.

Gloria shook her head. "I love spending time with him. I miss him..."

Briella grabbed some tissues from the marble tissue holder sitting on the countertop. "Come on, Gloria. Pull yourself together."

Gloria sniffled into the wad of tissues in her hand. "That's what everyone keeps telling me."

"You can scream and yell at my father all you want once we're gone. Don't let him get to you. He's an absolute arse and everyone knows it."

"Sometimes I think he forgets."

Briella smiled. "That he's an arse, or that he's got responsibilities? To be fair to him, he went so many years having hardly any responsibilities, then suddenly he's got a wife and three babies."

"He was better before..."

"What's that?"

Gloria shook her head. "Nothing. Shall we start a movie while we wait? I could go ahead and pop some corn. Could be our appetizer."

Briella went to the living room to find a film while Gloria got out a pan, oil, and corn kernels.

She was salting the freshly popped corn when the elevator doors finally dinged and out stepped Henry into the foyer of the penthouse.

Gloria added the popcorn pan to the sink and quickly ran some water into it before she headed to the living room to greet—and likely glare at—her husband.

"Daddy!"

He scooped Eva up. "Hello, darling. How've you been?"

"I missed you! We were watching a movie while we were waiting for you."

"Hi, Daddy," Charlotte said, stepping up and kissing his cheek.

"You've grown."

"I hope not," Charlotte said. "I'm nineteen."

"You might do some growing yet," Henry said. "You certainly are growing more lovely. You look just like your mother at your age."

Gloria flinched, and she noticed Briella glance over at her. She remained pinned in place, staring at the familial scene unfolding in front of her, feeling as though she didn't belong.

In her own home. That *she* had paid for.

The dinner that she had cooked for *his* children.

She felt sick.

She finally turned away, figuring she could go ahead and start setting the table and taking the food out. After all, dinner was already running behind, and she didn't want her babies to stay up too late. Besides, it was clear she had no place or purpose, beyond fixing dinner and taking care of everyone.

Gloria knew she was feeling sorry for herself, but she was devastated over what Henry had said about Charlotte being lovely and looking like her mother at her age...Gloria was already insecure about the relationship Henry had with his first wife, the history they shared.

Moments later, she heard Henry say, "Go help Gloria. She's already prepared all the food, she shouldn't have to set the table as well."

Charlotte and Brett came in and began setting the table, as Briella began carrying in the casserole dishes and bowls of food.

"Gloria."

She reluctantly returned to the living room, looking up into Henry's eyes, licking her lip nervously.

"Why are you looking at me like that, babygirl?" he asked, placing his finger under her chin and lifting her face to meet his gaze.

Mrs. Alexander had moved into the dining room to get the twins and Eva set up for dinner, so she and Henry were alone in the living room.

"You...you were late," she whispered.

"I'm sorry, baby. I couldn't leave until James was ready to go. He drove us there."

She frowned, glancing away from him. She was afraid to make him angry in front of their families.

“Well, baby, I don’t know what else you want from me. Didn’t I do what I told you I would do? I’m here, aren’t I?”

“You’re late,” she repeated, albeit timidly.

“Gloria, I’m doing my fucking best, alright? You had the car.”

“I was shopping with *your* daughter, Henry!” Gloria said, fiercely but quietly. She didn’t need anyone to hear their argument.

"So you were doing *me* the fucking favor then, were you?" he demanded. "Shall I simply inform my eldest that you were doing her a favor?"

"No, Henry." Gloria bit down hard on her lip. "Why are you being cruel?"

"Why are you trying to make me feel guilty?"

"Because you let me down," she whispered. "Do you have any idea how badly it hurts me when you do this? When you spend more time at the pub than you do with your family, your daughters? Me?"

Henry didn't answer right away; instead, he looked down at their feet, his trainers rather than dress shoes. He wasn't dressed for dinner as they'd agreed, but she didn't want to have to wait for him to get himself together, making dinner even later than it already was looking to be.

Finally he met her eyes, and the words he spoke hit Gloria at her very core. "You're nagging me as much as my ex-wife did before we divorced."

Gloria knew for a fact that Vic had been the one to divorce Henry, but it seemed Henry was doing everything in his power that evening to hurt her, to make her doubt them, their marriage, their relationship.

He'd already made her feel insecure about Vic...why was he going on that way?

Was he truly *that* angry with her? And if so, why?

"Henry..."

"What do you actually want from me, Gloria?" he asked, out of patience.

"I want you to be my husband."

"I am." He grabbed her face in his hand, making her look at him as he said, "I even dropped your laptop at the repair shop. That guy who works there is the biggest arse to deal with, but I did it for you, Gloria, because I know how important it is to you to write another damn book."

Gloria felt her face get hot. "I thought you like my books, baby?"

"Why are we even fighting?" he asked, snaking an arm around her waist and drawing her close, kissing her head. He knew how to get out of trouble with her; he was a mastermind, and Gloria was helpless as ever to her husband's well-honed charms. They seemed to work exclusively on her. She would have been surprised if any other woman in London could manage to find her Henry charming.

"I love you, Gloria," he said, his voice deep and low, in the way that made her pussy clench deliciously. "I can't wait until everyone goes to bed later, and I get to take you to ours, and to take what's mine, to show you just how much I appreciate you and love you, and how grateful I am to you for preparing this dinner for my family."

Gloria sighed. "It still hurts me that you can't seem to take our lives together seriously. I don't always want to come second to the pub. Baby, I told you I'd give you the freedom you crave...but you've sometimes got to show up for me, too."

"I've shown up for you," he said. "What am I missing? What am I doing wrong?"

Gloria took her husband's hand. "Come, we've delayed dinner long enough. I want my babies in bed before midnight."

He allowed her to guide him into the kitchen, but Gloria could sense his reluctance. She knew he likely didn't want to have dinner anymore, but surely he wanted the holiday with his *other* children? Those whom he rarely saw, save the holidays in which Gloria opened her home and slaved for days readying their home and the meal? Did he think she was doing so for *herself*?

All throughout the meal, Brett was complementary to the point Henry told him to stop hitting on his stepmother, which embarrassed everyone, but at least Henry was being somewhat sociable.

Finally, Briella and Brett cleaned up the kitchen while Henry, Gloria, Mrs. Alexander, Eva, Cheye, Charlotte, and Jem went into the living room to watch the film; once dinner was put away, they'd bake the cookies so that the babies could go down as soon as possible for their sleep.

The rest of the evening went well. The cookies were a hit, and sweet Charlotte helped get little Eva ready for bed so Gloria and Mrs. Alexander could take care of the twins.

Gloria allowed Henry to remain in the living room with Brett and Brielle, but they *would* be having a talk that evening about Henry's behavior. With Mrs. Alexander planning to head home soon so she could be back in Atlanta for Christmas, Gloria and Henry were going to be on their own with the twins and Eva again soon. Gloria was *not* willing to make all the sacrifices, giving up her writing time on the book she'd finally been able to make so much progress on without Henry making some sacrifices, too...especially since he was pressuring her for another pregnancy.

And especially, *especially,* since he should have given up the pub before he even dreamed of asking his wife to give up her writing *career.* After all, how did he expect them to keep their lifestyle without her doing some more work and publishing another book? Sure, the royalties on those she'd already published were good, but wouldn't keep them living high in London forever...

Gloria snuck away from her family while the older children were having dessert and talking to their father...and Mrs. Alexander had gone down to hers for a much-needed night of rest without the babies.

She had been putting it off all day, but it was time that she finally finish her confrontation with Dean.

7

Chapter Seven

She'd been dreading it all day, but as much as a huge part of her wanted to cut him off and never speak again—preserving her marriage to Henry—she knew she didn't have it in her to be cruel to him.

Gloria saw her most recent message from Dean, sent only a half hour earlier, which meant he had been messaging her nonstop, all day. Dean had been consistent from the beginning; he had never given up.

He would be the end of her...or, at least, the end of her shaky marriage, if she wasn't careful.

She wanted to be careful. She was terrified of losing Henry. She wanted to be with him for the rest of her life. If that meant giving him more babies, so be it.

She'd always wanted only two children, but as Henry had told her from the beginning that he wanted a big family...Gloria wouldn't mind having the same.

She took a deep breath, gathering all the courage she possessed as she hit the video call button on her phone.

Before the first ring had ended, Dean answered.

Gloria took a deep breath to steel herself, knowing she had to do everything in her power to not allow him to break her down.

"Why have you been calling and messaging me all day, Dean?" she asked. "I told you my husband's family were coming over today. I had to prep, and his oldest daughter and I went shopping together."

"And you didn't have five minutes out of your *busy* day to talk to me? We left things horrible between us, Gloria." He hesitated, taking a deep breath before he said, "and I'm in love with you."

Gloria raked the fingers of her free hand through her hair. "No, babe, you're not. You enjoy my company, and you're unhappy in your relationship with your girlfriend—"

"Gloria, I can't lose you."

"That's just the thing though. I am not yours to lose. I have a husband. I'm in love with him, and we have three babies together."

"So what are you doing with me, then?" Dean demanded. "Do you have any idea what I'm risking, having this relationship with you?"

"All the fights and the one-sided sex, you mean?"

"One-sided?" Dean demanded.

"You don't know that I've been faking it for the past few weeks? Since you got so damn demanding and wanting it all the time? What happened to the affection and the intimate conversation? When was the last time that you talked low and dirty to me?" Gloria demanded. "You always want me to do all the work. You get upset with me when I ignore you so I can write. Or spend time with my children.

"I'm a grown woman with a family and a career. I don't have time to entertain you, in exchange for you not getting angry with me."

Their relationship had stopped benefiting Gloria long before. He used to take his time with her, feeding her beautiful compliments, giving her what Henry never cared to.

Now he was as bad as Henry, always wanting his own needs met...not caring if Gloria was faking. Surely he wasn't foolish enough to believe all those moans during their video chat sessions had been sincere.

Then again, from Gloria's experience, once a woman started moaning, that was an aphrodisiac for men, and nothing else mattered at that point, other than nutting.

"What the fuck are you talking about?" Dean demanded.

"You're lazy in bed!"

He stared at her angrily, a look of betrayal across his face. "How can you say that? Fuck, Gloria!" he shouted.

"If you're going to scream at me, I'm ending this call. If you can't speak kindly and respectfully to me, then we're done here."

She was halfway hoping he would decide to end things with her so that she wouldn't have to. She also knew it was a stupid fear, but he'd been a fan of her writing—so he claimed—so what if he decided to expose their relationship?

What if he blackmailed her or hurt her career?

She wanted to believe he was more trustworthy than that, after all the conversations and intimacy and video sex they'd shared, but she knew better than to trust a lover.

But Dean switched things up, yet again...he had a way of doing that, a way of blowing past any expectations Gloria may have had. He always knew how to reel her back in.

"I'm so sorry."

Dean's words gave Gloria pause. "What?"

Dean nodded. "I'm sorry I spoke cruelly to you. You're the sweetest woman ever. You don't deserve that."

She slightly smiled. "I don't know about that."

"About what, sweetheart?" he asked, in that voice that made her melt.

"Me being the sweetest."

"Of course you are. Why wouldn't you think so?"

"Dean..."

And just like that, Gloria knew that she was going to forgive him.

"I'll do anything for you."

"What about your girlfriend?" she asked.

"I want you. God, baby, I wish we'd met years ago. We belong together."

She swallowed...even Henry had never told her that. Henry hadn't a romantic bone in his body. But Dean...for better or worse, knew what to say. He could sweep her off her feet with one sentence.

"I love you," he whispered.

"...fuck."

"Baby," he whispered, "I wish I was there with you. Makeup sex is the best sex, after all. And I miss your sweet pussy."

"You're going to have to work for it."

She enjoyed feeling that bit of power...knowing he was going to have to grovel after what he'd done to her, after how cruel he'd been. She was going to make *him* beg for it, turning the tables on him.

"I want you to sweet-talk me the way you used to," Gloria said, biting her lip as she looked into his eyes, through the miles and through the screen.

"Baby, I always—"

"No," she stated simply, reaching down to remove her panties from beneath her dress. "You've been slacking, and that's not you. You're not lazy. You're not going to stop trying to win me over just because you've got me now."

Dean gave her a sexy smile. "I have you?"

"For now," she said, still playing hard to get.

She wasn't ready to give him everything yet; he was going to have to prove himself before she would let her guard down again.

Of course, she had her panties off and her own cum slowly seeping down her inner thigh, so she wasn't sure how much more 'down' her guard could possibly be...

"Can I see how wet you are for me?" Dean asked, licking his lips hungrily.

Gloria felt wrong for it, knowing her husband was in the house, that he could step inside the closet she'd snuck into to talk to Dean. All she'd intended to do was talk.

Apparently, Gloria wasn't any more done with Dean than he had been with her, since she was in her closet, her pussy dripping as she lifted her dress over her hips and spread her thighs, pointing the camera up at her wetness.

"Oh, *fuck,* baby. You're so wet."

"Mmmhmmm. Tell me what you want to do to me. I'm your little fucktoy. How are you gonna use me?"

Thankfully, Dean didn't disappoint that time; it was almost as though he knew that the stakes were too high for him to let her down.

His voice was low, guttural, in a way that made her leak even more.

"I need you here to lap it all up, Daddy," Gloria said.

That was one of their things...she'd started calling him "Daddy" and he hadn't minded...none of her other lovers had been okay with it or into it, when it was a huge weakness for Gloria.

Henry wouldn't allow her to call him anything other than his name...never had.

"I love the way your pussy tastes," Dean muttered. "Spread your legs and touch your cunt."

Gloria moaned as her fingers brushed against her hot flesh, closing her eyes, giving herself over to complete ecstasy.

"I need you, Gloria."

"I need you, too."

She moved away from her phone, setting it up so Dean could watch her when she got back. She planned on putting on a show for him.

She kept her plethora of sex toys hidden away from prying eyes, in various places throughout the master suite...in her bedside table, in her second from the top bathroom vanity door, and in the drawers of her custom-made closet.

She crawled—somewhat awkwardly, due to her panties around her ankles and her dress bunched up around her waist—to one such drawer, digging out one of her nicest vibrators, one that was rechargeable, red in color, with a nicely curved handle. It felt great against her clit, but it felt *incredible* when she slipped it inside her, where her vaginal walls clung to it tightly, where it hit her g spot deeply and delectably.

Gloria crawled carefully back to her phone, putting on a performance for Dean.

She was blurring the lines, being questionably faithful to her husband. Of course, what she was doing wasn't right, but it wasn't as though she and Dean were actually sleeping together...he hadn't touched her.

Gloria smiled as she lay on her back in front of her propped-up phone, spreading her legs and switching on her vibrator.

"Good girl," Dean said, reaching into his pants and jerking on his cock a few times. "God, I need to bury my cock inside your tight little hole."

Gloria moaned, biting her lip as she looked into Dean's eyes as she pressed her vibrator against herself.

Gloria threw her head back...it had been a long time since she'd masturbated. Masturbating was supposed to be about personal pleasure, everything done to get oneself off, *not* doing it in order to please anyone else.

But Gloria was so turned on, and the vibrator felt *so fucking* ***good*** against her hypersensitive flesh, that she knew she could not stop, even if she'd wanted to.

"Imagine my fingers against your wet lips," Dean whispered.

Gloria whimpered, then she heard his fly unzipping; she opened her eyes and looked back at her phone screen, seeing Dean stand up to remove his trousers, then his briefs, his cock springing free.

Gloria had seen his cock before, but she could never get over the sheer *size* of it. Henry's wasn't small, but at seven inches, it wasn't massive.

Dean's cock had to be at least ten inches...maybe even larger. She'd never fucked a cock as big as his, and she was almost glad that they were only fucking over video chat. She was afraid he would be too much for her to take.

"I love your sweet cunt."

Gloria moaned softly. "I want to wrap my fingers around your massive cock. Daddy, I need it."

"Your Daddy wants to give you this massive cock. I want to feed it into your tight little pussy, inch by inch, until I'm all the way inside you, buried balls-deep."

She moaned. "Fuck."

"Yes, baby, I'm going to fuck you senseless, until all you can do is moan, all you can think about is my cock filling you up."

"Yes," Gloria moaned, throwing her head back, closing her eyes as she allowed her sensitive body to absorb the waves of pleasure echoing throughout her.

"Mmm, more, Daddy," she whispered.

"Put your fingers to your lips and get them nice and wet...I want you to taste yourself."

Gloria reached down to stroke her velvety pussy lips, gathering her own lubricant onto her fingers.

Once her fingers were sufficiently wet, she looked through the screen into Dean's eyes as she brought her fingers up to her mouth, sucking them, moaning at her own taste.

Dean moaned in response. "That's it, babygirl. Such a good girl for Daddy, aren't you?"

"I'm a good little slut," she whimpered.

"Yes, baby."

Suddenly Gloria had an idea...she knew what she had to do, because if Dean wasn't open to the type of play she liked best, then why was she risking her marriage to have video sex and an online relationship with him?

"Daddy?" she asked, a bit nervous.

"What, baby?" Dean asked, in his deep, raspy voice that tore Gloria apart at her very seams.

"I want you to call me a whore."

He hesitated. "Baby, I respect the hell out of you—"

"I want you to respect me...just not in bed, not while we're playing like this," Gloria whispered.

"Are you sure, Gloria?"

"I'm positive. Call me a whore. Tell me all the depraved things you want to do to me...right now, I'm your filthy slut. I want you to treat me like one."

She looked up into his eyes, watching him on the screen. Gloria could tell he had been holding back for so long. He'd wanted to devour her, to make her his, to mark her as his own from the beginning, but he'd been too much of a gentleman, first pretending to respect that Gloria was married, now pretending that he respected her as a human.

Gloria had been around the block enough times to know better: any man presented with the opportunity to be as depraved with a woman as he wanted to be, would do so with no holds barred, damning the consequences.

As long as their love affair remained online, there *were* no consequences, so long as Henry never got wind of it.

"I'm going to pin you to my bed and make you take every inch of my monster cock," Dean said, growling at her as he spoke.

"Mmm, tell me how it feels," she moaned, arching her back hard as a wave of pre-orgasmic ecstasy rolled over her.

"Your cunt is so tight it almost hurts," he moaned, and Gloria looked up at her phone screen just as Dean flexed his hips, and she could almost *feel* his massively thick cock filling her to the brim, making her feel fuller than she'd ever been.

"Oh, god," Gloria moaned. "Fuck, that feels so good."

"You like this cock, whore?"

"Mmm, Daddy, I love your cock," she whimpered, slipping her vibrator inside. Gloria was so wet she didn't even need to lube her toy at all. It slipped right in, as turned on as Dean had made her.

"Oh, god, Gloria, that was fucking hot," he moaned. "Pull that vibrator back out and shove it right back inside. I want to see you penetrated again."

Her vibrator felt amazing inside her, its contours hitting her walls and that magic spot just right. She whimpered in frustration as she did as he told her and removed the toy, and her sopping pussy made a wet noise that made Dean's cock give a huge jolt.

Gloria thought Dean was going to cum, but at the last moment he stopped himself, and instead he groaned. "Fuck yourself hard."

Gloria pressed her vibrator back inside; it didn't feel nearly as good that time since she wasn't as wet, her toy having absorbed some of her lubricant before she pulled it out and forced it back in. Dean had lost points with that move.

"I love fucking you," he moaned, stroking his huge cock in long, hard strokes. Gloria wished he would speed things up, because she'd wanted a quick, hard, rough fuck, to come hard and violently, then for it to be over. Soon Henry would be coming to bed. They still needed to have that conversation about why he'd been late for dinner, but fucking Dean beforehand had been exactly the stress-relief Gloria needed in order to be able to handle everything else that came her way that evening.

"Fuck me harder and faster, Daddy," Gloria whimpered, desperately wanting him to fill her with his 'seed.'

She needed to come, and she wanted him to cum as quickly as possible; she'd loved the pace that the two of them had set early on in their affair, about five minutes of foreplay and ten minutes of 'fucking' before they came at the same time...she knew every time the two of them fucked couldn't be perfect, but she missed the days when he'd seemed to be unable to stop himself from cumming, when he had exploded as soon as she'd begun moaning...when her moans had been sincere, unstoppable.

"Dean, jack yourself faster," Gloria said, breaking character as she sat up and looked at him.

"I like the pace we're going at."

She bit her lip. "I want it harder."

Dean sighed; Gloria could tell she was taking him out of the moment, but *she'd* been out of it for a few minutes by that point, and she didn't think it was fair if she had to be the one left unsatisfied.

Instead, she thought about how he was watching her, the power it gave her, and she moaned loudly—likely too much so—as she arched her back and wiggled her hips so her vibrator hit inside her just right, sending her over the edge, making her cum hard.

She heard Dean grunt as he too came, and she was about to watch the cum shooting from his dick, when she heard footsteps coming from her bedroom, followed seconds later by the sound of Henry entering her closet, where her lewd behavior was still on full display...

It would have been easy to expose what she was doing, having online sex with a man she'd become close with behind her husband's back, but instinct took over and—*not* wanting to get caught—Gloria pushed her phone into the back of her closet, just as Henry stepped inside.

"What're you up to in here, all alone, babygirl?" Henry asked, looking at Gloria like he wanted to eat her alive, having spotted her in her closet masturbating.

He never would have suspected that someone else was involved.

"Um...just..."

"I can see what you're doing, babygirl. Why did you get started without me?"

Before Gloria could react, Henry was knelt between her legs, his tongue against her clit while the toy still pulsed deep inside her. She knew Dean was still on the phone, that he could hear what was going on, but Henry's tongue felt so fucking *good* against her clit that she could care about little else as she gave into the intense and unbelievable pleasure of what Henry's mouth was capable of, combined with the delicious feel of the vibrator deep inside her.

"I wonder what would happen if I..."

For a moment, Gloria feared Henry was going to pull the vibrator out. She was so close to orgasm, though, that she would have died if he took it away from her.

Instead, Henry effortlessly flipped her over and spread her legs so she was on her belly. She knew exactly what he was wanting as she arched her back and lifted her ass into the air, widening her legs to give him the best access possible to her asshole.

"Good girl," he said, spitting on her hole and rubbing more of his spit on his cock. Seconds later, Gloria was impaled in her ass, making her jolt forward on her hands and knees as he split her open.

She was fuller than she could remember being, her ass full of Henry and her pussy full of her vibrator, shoved deep inside her, to its hilt.

Henry fucked her in deep, slow strokes as he reached back and hit the button on her toy until the vibrator was going at full force, then he reached forward between her legs as he began stroking her clit, matching the pace of his thrusts.

It was moments before Gloria felt a massive orgasm building deep inside her. The combined pressure of the vibrator against her g spot and her husband's cock driving it even deeper, along with the way he was playing with her clit, created the most incredible orgasm of Gloria's life, as she came apart with Henry buried balls-deep inside her, as her ass and pussy both clenched and throbbed, and her knees gave out underneath her.

Henry hadn't cum yet, so he kept going, kept hammering away at her, not letting up on the vibrator either as he fucked her so hard that she had another orgasm just as Henry grunted and moaned as he shot stream after stream of his hot cum deep inside her.

"Fuck. I love you, Gloria," Henry said, taking her shoulders gently as he rolled her over onto her back so she was looking up at him.

Gloria bit her lip as she looked lovingly into Henry's eyes, sighing happily as he leaned in and kissed her lips, softly.

"I love you, baby," she moaned, when their lips parted.

Dean was all but forgotten; in fact, there was a part of Gloria that was glad that he'd heard her fucking Henry, that Henry had interrupted what they'd been doing.

Gloria wanted to stay with Henry. Leaving him had never *truly* been a consideration, no matter how nice Dean had made that idealistic life between the two of them sound...the life that never could have happened.

Dean had been a distraction, but Henry...he was hers, her husband, the man she'd fought for, the love of her life.

If she kept Dean at a distance, everything between her and Henry would be okay.

"Gloria?" He ran his fingers through her hair, across her face, then down her back, making her arch hard, pressing back up against him, where he was still buried deep inside her.

"You feel so good and tight around me."

She smiled against his mouth as he leaned over her, pressing his lips to hers tenderly.

"It's because you made me cum so hard," she whispered, taking his handsome face in her hands as she looked into his deep brown eyes.

"Yeah?"

"Mmm," Gloria moaned. "*And* because I love you so much."

"I love you, too."

He kissed her mouth, then her forehead. He then stood, holding his hand down to her, helping her to her feet. "I'm not done with you yet, babygirl. Ready for Round Two?"

8

Chapter Eight

Henry made gentle, sweet love to Gloria in their bed...so tenderly she was in tears after their simultaneous orgasms.

Henry had insisted—back when they'd first begun sleeping together—that he couldn't be satisfied by tender, soft sex. Now though, Gloria knew it wasn't true. She also knew Henry loved her deeply and entirely.

She was so filled with regret and pain that she couldn't hold it in anymore. There was no way in hell she could lie to her Henry.

"Baby," she said, between tears.

"There's no way that I hurt you," he said, looking horrified.

He usually liked hurting her...she wasn't sure what that meant, what was going on with him or with *them* to cause such a shift. Was it all because she'd been entertaining another man on the side? Was her own guilt getting to her, making her see that she had a good man all along—with his flaws, of course, but Gloria's flaws were just as severe—and to show her how tender he could truly be, that there was nothing she needed from Dean that Henry wasn't more than capable of giving her?

"No, you didn't hurt me at all...that was incredible, Henry." She swallowed hard, then choked back a sob as she said, "I love you so much!"

"Aww, baby," he said, gathering her close and pulling her against him tightly. "It's okay. I'm here, and I love you."

She buried her face against his chest. "I love you more than anything."

Henry trailed his fingers through her hair. "I know you do." He took her face in his hands, looking into her eyes for a few moments before he leaned in and deeply kissed her mouth. He didn't kiss her like he was trying to have sex again, but in a way that made her feel safe, protected, cherished, and loved.

It made Gloria cry even harder. She shed tears of guilt and heartbreak, because she knew it was going to destroy Dean when she completely cut him off, and she hated the idea of hurting him, but she wasn't willing to risk Henry for anything.

"Baby, please don't cry," Henry said, gentle humor in his voice as he kissed the top of her head. "Everything is good."

She wrapped her arms around him. "I just need you."

"I'm here," he said, stroking long, gentle passes over her bare back. "My beautiful babygirl."

Gloria sighed. She'd *never* felt that close to him, that safe, that loved by him. She'd never thought she and Henry could be that close. There had been a part of her that had wondered if she could have found that sweet, caring closeness in Dean's arms, but with his obsessive and controlling nature, he scared her at times, in a way far more sinister than anything Henry had done. While Henry was a complete ass at times, she felt he was stable, at least.

Dean, on the other hand, was as unstable as Gloria. Maybe that meant they deserved each other—it wasn't exactly fair for Henry to be stuck with a basket case for a wife, no matter how Gloria took care of him and loved him—but she knew she would fight to the death to remain with Henry.

Extricating herself from Dean was going to be the issue.

"Are you sure that you're okay, Gloria?"

Everything inside her longed to confess her "affair" to her husband, but she also remembered hearing, long before, that men *never* wanted to know about their wives or girlfriends stepping out on them, that they'd rather live in denial.

Gloria was going to do everything in her power to make sure Henry never found out. Although she hadn't had physical sex with Dean, he had nudes and videos of her, and they had an emotional connection.

"Would you tell me what's going on with you?" Henry asked. "I thought I'd made it up to you, for being late for dinner."

Gloria brought her hands up to the back of his neck, cupping the back of his head gently in her hands. "I'm not upset with you in the least, Henry. I love you. I think you're the best husband and father in the world, I'm so sorry if I ever acted like I didn't feel that way—"

"Gloria," he finally said, "please calm yourself, take a breath. You're not making any sense...you're not having an attack, are you?" he asked, concerned.

Gloria shook her head. "Well, I am having an anxiety attack, but that's not my problem. I'm just...I'm dealing with some things."

A dark expression passed over Henry's face. "Briella mentioned that she discussed something upsetting with you today."

Gloria met his eyes. "You mean my uncle."

He nodded, his gaze never straying from hers.

"That's...that's not the issue," she said, having to glance away in shame.

Sweetly—and in a way that made Gloria's eyes fill with tears of both grief and gratitude—Henry stroked her cheek. "Don't be ashamed of what that man did to you. You have nothing to be ashamed of, my darling."

She started crying harder. She'd made such a mess of things. She'd learned years ago that, no matter what had happened to her in the past, her life was for living, but she was doing a terrible job at it.

"Gloria," Henry said, looking sternly into her eyes, "I'm going to need you to speak to me here, and to tell me what it is you're thinking. What's going on with you, babygirl? Why are you crying as though your heart is broken?"

She wrapped her arms tightly around him. "It makes me emotional when you make love to me that way. It makes me feel like..." she trailed off though, staring up into his eyes.

"Like what, babygirl?'

"Like you love me."

"Surely you don't doubt that?"

"No," she said, although it was a bit of a lie on her part, "but sometimes when we have sex—when you fuck me, Henry—it makes me feel like you straight up *hate* me."

"I've never hated you. That's just how I fuck, and you know that. You used to like it," he said, sounding almost wistful as he held her and kissed her forehead.

"I know. I do like it. I just...I guess I need more reassurance." She stroked his face tenderly, running her fingers through his hair as she went on to say, "I need you to make love to me more, and to act as though you actually enjoy it.

"And I need you to sleep beside me every night. I need you, all the time. I can't live without you, Henry. Not in any way."

He pulled her closer, so she was lying directly on top of him, the way Henry knew she loved to sleep.

"I'll do better. I can't lose you either, Gloria. Seeing you in the closet, pleasuring yourself like you had to hide from me, to hide your *pleasure* from me...that fucking hurt."

"I didn't mean to hurt you." She bit down hard on her lip. "I *love you,* Henry!"

"I love you too, babygirl. And you didn't hurt me. It hurt to know that you had to hide from me in order to get yourself off. Do I ever get you off anymore?"

"Oh, baby, of course you do. All the time. You're amazing in bed."

"Am I?"

She kissed him hard. "Just now...you felt how fucking hard I came."

"I did, baby."

"You don't think that I could have fucking faked *that,* do you?"

He smiled. "Babygirl, I hope you've never faked it with me. Do you know how much I love you?"

She smiled. "Yes."

He sighed. "I'll always love you."

She swallowed hard. "No matter what?"

"Marriage is unconditional love, babygirl. If I hadn't loved you that way, I wouldn't have made you my wife."

Gloria gasped, then she wrapped her arms tightly around his back as she tangled her legs around his waist, reaching up to press her forehead against his, closing her eyes. "Henry, you have no idea what you do to me."

"The same that you do to me. You think I'd be this whipped for anyone else in this whole fucking world, Gloria? I had to go out of the country to find a woman who affects me as deeply as you do."

She smiled, then opened her mouth as he began to kiss her. She moaned as he pressed his tongue inside her mouth.

"Mmm, that's right, baby. Moan into my mouth. Show me how good it feels."

Gloria whimpered as he entered her again, as he slowly, deeply began fucking her. It didn't take him long to get her right on the edge, then he pulled back, easing slightly out of her.

She bit her lip as she looked up at him. "Henry, please don't tease me right now."

"You love edging."

"I love *you,*" she whispered as she leaned up to claim his mouth.

Henry moaned against her neck as he lowered his body over hers and began hammering her, deep strokes that made her weak.

"I love you too," he said, pinning her down with his strong body over hers as he thrust deeper. "You like me hitting you that deep?"

"Y-yes," Gloria stuttered, so close to cumming she couldn't think of much else.

"Fuck, I love you," he said, grunting as he breathed hard, reaching down to put both of his hands on her left hip as he shoved her legs wider apart.

"I can't take much more," she whimpered as he fucked her.

"You take it until I say you're done and I let you cum," Henry said. "Remember who you belong to, babygirl."

Gloria's heart lurched as his words hit her as deeply as he was fucking her...*she was his.*

But he hadn't been acting that way lately, had he? He was there on top of her, fucking her for all he was worth, telling her he loved her and she belonged to him...and as into it as Gloria was, she was still thinking about Dean, about how she was breaking his heart as she lay underneath her husband...

"Mmm, good girl," Henry moaned, kissing her. He wrapped his fingers around her neck, keeping his cock buried to the hilt inside her. He slightly pulled back, looking into her eyes, and she could tell from the way he looked at her just how much he cared for her, how he craved her...it was addictive.

She'd never wanted anything more than to have him inside her, in that moment. She wanted him to make her forget her guilt.

"Henry."

"Yes, babygirl?" Henry continued to fuck her like he wasn't on the edge, like he wasn't about to cum all inside her, although Gloria could tell from the way he was breathing, how his eyes rolled back in his head, and from the sheer amount of sweat dripping down his body and onto hers, that it was taking everything he possessed not to shoot his seed inside her at that very moment.

"I want you to put a baby inside me tonight."

Henry groaned, then laughed as he licked her neck. "You really want my cum, don't you, babygirl?"

"I do. I love you. I want us to have more babies."

His lips found hers. He kissed her long and hard, then he pulled back, breathless.

"Fuck, baby. I'm going to cum."

"Yes," Gloria moaned, throwing her head back against the pillows.

"Cum with me, babygirl. Clench that tight cunt around my cock as I pump my seed into your ovaries."

He leaned his head down, pressing his forehead against her shoulder as he fucked her even harder and deeper...one, two more strokes, and they were both shaking from the effort of holding back from their orgasms.

He grunted, then said, “Cum for me, baby.”

Gloria whimpered, then let out a loud moan as she gave into her orgasm. Her entire body trembled and shook as she came with an explosive orgasm, one so intense it reverberated throughout her body.

Henry placed his hand over her mouth as she came so she wouldn’t scream out loud and wake the whole house. She clenched even harder as Henry bit her neck, then licked the soreness away.

She was still twitching and shaking. “I love you,” she whispered, wrapping as tightly around Henry as she could, clinging aggressively to him like she would never let him go.

He rolled her over, so she was on top of him. As nice as it had been, she hoped he wasn’t wanting a round three, though, because she was sore and entirely spent.

But he held her face in his hands as he looked into her eyes. “I love you, beautiful.”

Gloria smiled happily. “I love you, handsome.”

“Fuck.”

Gloria kissed him, then she laid her head on his chest, grateful when he began stroking her back, keeping his cock buried deep inside her.

“I bet I just knocked you up.”

Gloria laughed. “I hope so.”

Henry trailed his fingers through her hair. “Are you sure that’s really what you want? I know you were on the fence earlier.”

Gloria hadn’t been on the fence. She’d been positive that she was done. She was barely able to handle the three she already had.

But she felt so bad for what had happened...surely guilt wasn’t a good reason for bringing another human into the world, but all Gloria had to do was think about how much she loved Henry, how much she loved the life they’d built and the family they had created...

And not only was she then willing to give Henry everything, but she was also happy to do whatever Henry wanted.

Eventually, Henry fell asleep that night beside her, where he belonged; Gloria only wished that she'd been able to enjoy the sweet moment more, that it hadn't been spoiled...not only by her guilt.

She hated herself for hurting Dean, no matter how incredible her night with Henry had been.

Once Henry fell asleep, Gloria thought about carefully climbing out of bed and tiptoeing into the closet, finding the phone she'd tossed, and calling Dean.

She knew he'd be upset, and he would do nothing to alleviate her guilt. He would try his hardest to make her feel even worse than she already did for what she'd done: committing the crime of sleeping with her own husband.

She curled into Henry, burying her face against him. Even in his sleep, he tightened his arms around her, and Gloria sighed in satisfaction.

Henry made her feel safe. She'd been so close to confessing what she'd done, but she was also certain she'd made the right decision in not telling him about Dean.

What Henry didn't know could never hurt him.

Gloria knew she was going to be carrying that guilt around with her for the rest of her life...not to mention her guilt over hurting Dean.

She'd taken him back, they had reunited, then she'd gone and fucked her husband while Dean listened. Maybe he'd never want to speak to her again, anyway, and, well...as much as that truly *would* break Gloria's heart, she also knew her and Dean's relationship couldn't continue.

No matter how much she couldn't stop thinking about him, even lying curled up in Henry's arms.

9

Chapter Nine

As soon as Gloria woke the next morning, she glanced over at the clock on her bedside table, seeing it was still early enough for her to find her phone and call Dean. She took a deep, dread-filled breath, then carefully crawled out from under Henry's arm, strewn across her stomach.

Thankfully she managed to get out of bed without waking Henry. She stepped into her slippers before arranging the blankets over Henry. She knew covering her husband with blankets would not be enough to make up for leaving their bed to phone another man, even though she was ending her relationship with Dean when she called.

On shaking legs, she found her robe and wrapped it around herself before she walked quietly into her closet, shutting the door silently before turning on the light.

First, she saw the pile of clothing—both hers and Henry's—strewn across the closet floor from where they'd frantically stripped down the evening prior. She glanced toward the corner of her closet where she'd tossed her phone and knelt, moving aside some clothing, hoping her phone wasn't shattered.

Finally she found it. She'd had it on video chat, and Dean had ended their chat at some point—thankfully—but Gloria still wondered how much of what had gone on between Gloria and Henry Dean had heard.

He'd sent her several messages and had tried to call her back on video chat for hours, as Gloria had expected. Although she felt bad for what she was about to do, she hated his incessant calls.

Gloria found her phone. She slipped out onto the balcony from her closet so she wouldn't wake her husband, especially not with the tears she knew would fall.

She had on only her pajamas and robe as she stepped onto the balcony, but she knew she couldn't be out there long. She had dressed—or underdressed, rather—accordingly, hoping the chill in the air would keep her from staying out too long.

After all, she was celebrating Christmas with her family. Dean, as much as she cared for him, and even *loved* him, he wasn't a part of that life, and he never *would* be.

Gloria had made her decision: Henry was it for her.

Dean's phone rang twice before he answered it. "Gloria?"

"Hi," she said, her voice soft, feeling both afraid and shy.

"What the hell happened last night?"

She took another breath. "Henry came into the closet while we were...you know."

"Gloria, I heard the two of you fucking."

"Yeah, we did."

"Did he hurt you?"

"No, of course he didn't *hurt* me—"

"How am I supposed to believe you, baby? You've not been shy about telling me all of the ways he's bullied and intimidated you."

"He's a good man."

"Why...why are you defending him to me, Gloria?" Dean asked, uneasy.

"Because... I'm sorry. I'm in love with Henry. He's my husband. I *fought* for him, you know? And we have a family...I can't keep doing this with you."

"What are you saying?"

"We've taken this too far. I told you from the beginning this didn't feel right to me."

"You kept talking to me."

"I know."

"You can't just end things with me."

"But I am. Dean, I *do* love you...but I won't destroy my family for you."

"I *loved* you."

"This hurts, but it's the right thing to do. It's what *must* be done, Dean. I'm sorry, but we've got to stop talking."

"Even as friends?" he asked.

Gloria halfway laughed. "Were we ever *just* friends?"

He was silent.

"Dean?"

"What do you want from me?" he asked, broken.

"I told you...I want to end this. I want to be with my husband."

"You don't love him."

"I do! I never said anything about not loving him—"

"He doesn't love *you,* Gloria."

"Don't you fucking say that," she said in a low voice.

"Why? Because you know it's true? The truth hurts, Gloria. You of all people know that, don't you?"

"What do you mean?"

"You lost your virginity to your uncle."

"Fuck!"

"Don't leave me. You know the only reason you wanted to be with Henry in the first place is because he's the first man who made you feel okay with your sexuality."

Gloria didn't respond...she was fuming—and deeply hurting—on the inside, but there was no use in having it out with Dean over the bullshit he was spewing. "I'm ending this, Dean. Nothing you say is going to change my mind."

"So we're wasting our time here, then?"

"I suppose," she whispered.

"Then what the fuck are we doing?"

Gloria bit down hard on her lip, then said, "I'm not sure. I'm sorry that it had to end this way. And I *do* love you, okay?"

"No," he said, suddenly softer, not hurling insults and accusations. "It's not okay at all."

Gloria did everything in her power to hold back her tears, knowing that ending the call as quickly as possible was her best bet. She swallowed her emotions as she said, "I've got to go, baby. Is there anything else you need to say to me?"

"You're really doing this, aren't you?" he demanded, insulted. "You're breaking up with me."

"Darling," Gloria said, "prolonging our breakup isn't going to make it any better. I will always love you and wonder about the life we could have had, but I've got to let you go.

"Go back to your girlfriend. She doesn't know anything about us, does she?"

Dean didn't respond.

"I'll go be with my husband, and soon, you'll forget I existed."

"You're my soulmate. I'll never forget you," Dean insisted. "Until the day that I die."

"I love you. Take care of yourself."

"Gloria, please."

"No, I've really got to go. Dean...I love you. Goodbye, baby."

She waited to see if he was going to say anything else, to try to keep her on the line longer. She wasn't cold enough to hang up on him.

Finally, he said, "Henry doesn't love you, and he'll destroy your life.

"Just know, Gloria, when that day comes, and you know it in your gut that you can't stay with him anymore, I'll be waiting."

She was silent for a few moments, with great reluctance allowing his words to sink in, before she said, "Okay. Thank you."

"I love you, babygirl. We *will* speak again. I'll always be here for you, okay?"

"Goodbye, Dean."

She waited.

Dean took a shaky breath, then said, "Talk soon, baby."

She hung up before she could say anything else, before she could get weak and beg for his forgiveness...before she could ask if they could keep talking to each other, to continue their affair, for what it was.

She knew she'd made the right decision, that she'd done the only thing that she *could* have done. Sticking with Dean would have been the nail in her own coffin.

She belonged to Henry, and to no one else, no matter how many men she'd been with, and no matter who had touched her, or who had seen her nude body. Henry was the one who had claimed her, who had made her his. She wanted no one else, no matter how deeply she and Dean had connected, no matter how sweet he had been.

They were over.

She was Henry's, end of story.

That didn't stop her, however, from barely being able to walk as she made her way back into her closet on shaking legs, as she tried not to allow the grief coursing through her veins to decimate her.

Gloria had felt so much heartache in her life but losing Dean—especially knowing that she was the one walking away from him, to think she was turning her back on the purest and most gentle love that had ever graced her life, cut deeply.

She fell to her knees on the hard marble floor, not caring that she'd have new bruises, not caring about anything, dead to any stimulus other than the intense pain radiating all throughout her body, coming straight from her heart, each time it beat.

She was having a hard time breathing. Gloria knew she needed to pull herself together. She had a Christmas celebration to host, and the children would be waking soon. She needed to be able to show up for her children, to be a selfless mother, as she'd promised herself she would be, from the moment she first held Eva in her arms.

She heard Henry moving around in their bedroom. Gloria quickly got up, heading for the bathroom and starting the shower. She didn't want Henry to see that she'd been crying, and to wonder what was wrong with her. Now that she'd finally managed to end things with Dean, the last thing Gloria needed was for Henry to figure out that there had been another man in her life.

Now, she wanted to focus all her love and affection on the one man she should have been giving it to.

But Dean...he'd almost been worth it.

Gloria was washing her hair when she heard Henry enter the bathroom. Moments later, the shower door opened, and she felt him standing behind her.

Her face was wet, but Gloria still didn't trust herself to present the portrait of a happy woman to Henry, so she kept her back turned toward him.

Then he wrapped his arms around her, and Gloria felt every part of her melting.

"Babygirl, are you okay?" he asked, holding her close, her back to his front.

She could feel his cock poking into her inner thigh, but she couldn't blame him for getting hard. He didn't know what she'd just been through, didn't know her heart was breaking—and he never *could* know the reason why—and she *was* nude inside the shower. It was natural that his cock would be hard enough to impale her at a moment's notice, if he even gave her that long.

Gloria knew she was going to have to give Henry sex. She wasn't feeling it, of course, but she couldn't have him knowing anything was wrong with her.

Henry surprised her, though, moving her hair to the side, over her shoulder, and gently kissing her neck.

Gloria sighed. "That feels so good, baby."

"Good," he said, running his hands down her back. He pulled her closer but simply held her, wrapping one arm around her neck to immobilize her, which would have been incredibly hot, had Gloria been in the mood.

"Henry," she whispered, bringing her hands up to rest on his arms, gently stroking them.

"What, babygirl?"

She breathed out deeply, then said, "I love you, so much."

He kissed her head. "I love you, baby."

She reached up, running her fingers through his hair.

Truthfully, he had no idea just how *much* she loved him.

Christmas was beautiful, and it went off without any struggle. Gloria was even able to pull her head out of her heartbreak, to focus on her family, on how happy her babies and her stepchildren were.

Charlotte was lovely, helping the twins with their presents since they were too small to open their own gifts, and they didn't understand what was going on, anyway. It was heartwarmingly cute, watching them look back and forth between each other every time one of their siblings squealed over a gift they opened. Their secret twin language was more a source of amusement than frustration for Gloria that day.

Eva sat happily on Briella's lap as she had already opened her gifts but was sleepy from having awakened so early. Gloria's mother had filmed the gift exchange on her phone and was now in the kitchen starting breakfast.

Gloria rested her head on Henry's shoulder, sighing happily. She truly *was* happy; she still felt guilty for breaking up with Dean, but she knew she was where she needed to be: with her family, and in the arms of the man she loved.

She was sitting on the sofa beside Henry as they watched Eva and Charlotte playing with one of the toys Eva had gotten.

Henry kissed her cheek, and she looked up into his eyes, smiling, almost overcome with the love she felt for him.

He lowered his mouth to her ear, then whispered, "By next Christmas, I want you to be sitting here with me, with our new baby in your arms...or, at the very least, inside your womb."

Gloria smiled, reaching up to kiss him. "Henry, I'm so in love with you."

He kissed her back, then said, "I love you, babygirl."

Nothing could have ruined that moment for Gloria...not the thought of her mother in the kitchen while Gloria sat for a few more blissful moments taking it all in.

The guilt still taking up residence inside Gloria's belly couldn't touch the bliss she was experiencing in that moment, nor could the jealous glances coming from Brett, which was so odd it made her uncomfortable...but not just then.

Because, on that Christmas morning, all Gloria cared about was her family.

Her sweet babies, and her Henry.

10

Chapter Ten

Henry's children had returned home late the night before, and Gloria's mother had decided to stay in the penthouse for a few days to help Gloria and Henry adjust to having the children all the time again. Gloria wasn't sure how she was going to have time to write now, but she was more concerned about spending time with her family...and with Henry.

She knew she *could* still write, so that fear had been faced and proven false. Now, all she was concerned with was making sure that first, her children were happy, and secondly, that she and Henry were doing well.

Having faced the possibility of losing Henry, Gloria now knew she would do anything in the world to make sure they never fell apart. He was her world, her heart and soul, and the love of her life. There was nothing she wouldn't do for him; she desperately hoped that she was already pregnant with their next child.

She would *not* lose him.

Gloria was making their bed late that afternoon when Henry came home. He'd gone to pick up her repaired laptop, which was a huge relief to Gloria. She at least needed her laptop within reach for when she found a moment to finish her book, which was nearing completion.

She was so excited for him to be home...she couldn't forget how affectionate and loving he'd been lately. After their sweet moment, dreaming together on the sofa the evening before about expanding their family, he'd taken her to bed and made love to her. He'd even seemed to be fully satisfied, even though the sex had been gentle and loving.

He was as fulfilled as she was.

He let himself into the bedroom. The second he was in her presence, Gloria knew something was wrong.

He was like a dark cloud descending upon her.

Slowly, she smoothed the comforter back in place as she turned to face him, swallowing hard when she saw the venomous look on his face.

She took a deep breath. "Are you okay?"

"You tell me, Gloria," he said, his voice so cold it sent a chill down her spine.

She halfway took a step toward him, but the menacing vibe radiating from him was enough to make her take two steps backward.

"Baby?" she asked, biting down hard on her lower lip.

"Is there something that you want to *tell* me, Gloria?"

"I don't know what you're talking about. What happened? Are you okay?"

He took a few long steps toward her, so aggressively Gloria shrank back against the wall in fear.

"Don't fucking give me that, you whore."

"W—what?" Gloria asked, her heart pounding so hard she thought it might burst out of her chest.

"I had to log onto your laptop at the shop, to make sure that it was working properly."

She nodded.

"Do you know where this is going?" Henry demanded.

"T—tell me."

He had her gold laptop under his arm. He opened it, scowling at the screen for a moment before he turned it toward Gloria. "Does this ring a fucking bell, slut?"

Gloria took a step closer to him so she could see the screen, knowing what she was going to see before Henry showed it to her, but she still had a difficult time forcing herself to look at her laptop screen.

Henry stepped forward and grabbed her face harshly in one hand, squeezing her chin. "Look at it, goddamn it! *You* did this, Gloria," he said, shaking his head. Then he glanced down, as though it were too painful for him to continue looking at his wife as he said, "*You* did this," more softly...and sounding broken.

Gloria choked on a sob...not because she was upset at being caught—although of course, that was a part of it—but because she was so deeply hurt by Henry's pain.

"You don't fucking get to cry, you whore!" Henry shouted, making Gloria flinch.

"H-Henry, I'm so, so sorry. Please, let me explain—"

"Explain *what,* exactly? That you were fucking another guy behind my back?"

"I wasn't fucking him. He never touched me. I've never even met him, baby."

Henry let go of her face and walked over to the dresser, where he placed her laptop down so carefully she *knew* he'd wanted to smash it to pieces.

Gloria took a few ragged breaths as she tried not to cry, although it was *all* she wanted to do, as her heart broke, knowing she'd just destroyed her marriage to the man she loved more than her own life, the man whom she had fought so hard to be with...

Her stifled sobs quickly turned to hyperventilating breaths, then gasps of surprise, then fear, as Henry closed the distance between them, grabbing her so hard that it hurt.

"Henry—"

"Shut up, Gloria! For once, shut the fuck up and listen to me."

She swallowed a whimper of primal fear. She had *never* seen her husband so angry and unhinged, and it terrified her.

"Listen to me, slut. You are nothing more than a wet hole to stuff my cock inside, do you know that?" He grabbed her by her throat, so hard she immediately started to choke. "I could replace you in a second. Don't think that you're special. There's a lot of cunts waiting for this meat here in London."

"I'm sorry. We just started talking, and—"

"Stop it, Gloria!"

She cried out in fear, but he tightened his grip around her neck so tightly that she couldn't breathe, let alone speak.

"No one cheats on me, do you understand? Especially not a weak little girl like you who cries every time I try to touch you." He leaned in, whispering into her ear, "I want the woman I married, not the woman you've become."

Despite her choking, Gloria began to cry at her husband's hurtful words, the fact he didn't love her. In that moment, she truly believed he'd never loved her at all, even though his actions up to that moment had proven otherwise, and he'd told her just the night before, as he'd made love to her, over and over, just how deeply he loved and adored her.

"Stop fucking crying, bitch!" Henry ordered, as he forced her back onto their bed and continued to hold her down and to choke her, harder and harder, until she was nearly blacking out.

Gloria's vision went grey, and she felt her life slipping away when Henry finally released his hold on her neck, and she was able to breathe.

"Think about how easily I could have killed you, Gloria," Henry said, as he leaned his weight on top of her, keeping her pinned down to their bed, helpless, even more so since he'd nearly choked the life out of her.

He didn't even *have* to pin her down to keep her from trying to get away from him, she was so weak. He felt the power he had over her, and he proceeded to use it to his advantage.

He wanted to put her in her place...to get revenge.

Revenge on her, on the only woman he'd ever truly loved, the only woman whom he would have allowed to reform him. He'd given her everything, and even *that* hadn't been enough for his whore of a wife.

She had broken him, so he fully intended to break her. Henry was mad with grief and the sting of betrayal. He wanted to break her so thoroughly that she would never want another man's touch...and Henry knew just how to do that.

He looked down at her, seeing that her own eyes were barely open, but he knew she was conscious, knew she was aware of everything happening...that she would know exactly what he was doing to her.

"You're mine." He reached down, yanking her leggings off, along with her panties, in one aggressive tug. "And I'm going to remind you of that."

He saw the realization dawn in her eyes, then the sheer terror in her gaze as she helplessly stared up at him.

Just to make sure that she didn't try to escape him, he kept one hand on her shoulder, forcing her harshly down on the mattress as he used his other hand to unzip his trousers...to tug his cock out of his underwear.

Gloria tried to brace herself for what she knew was about to happen...but again, she knew from experience that nothing could prepare her for the agony she was about to be forced to endure.

She began to cry silently, her throat too sore to make a sound, as she felt Henry force himself inside her, painfully impaling her. She whimpered in protest, trying to squirm away, but she also knew there was no escaping him, that he was going to have his way with her, and there was nothing she could do about it.

She stared up at the ceiling, willing the whole experience to be over; she felt her mind separating itself from her body, and she realized that staring at the ceiling was something all too familiar, reminding her of something that she'd spent almost two decades trying to forget.

"You like horses, don't you?"

Gloria was sitting in the passenger seat of her uncle's GMC Sierra; he'd swung by her house early afternoon that day, unannounced.

Gloria had been out by the pool, relaxing, when her father had come out the back door and yelled at her that her uncle was there.

Confused, as she hadn't been told that he was stopping by, Gloria stood from the chair she'd been lounging in, grabbing her cover-up and slipping her feet into her slides as she made her way to the house.

Sure enough, her uncle was seated at the breakfast bar, a beer in hand. Gloria had never felt uncomfortable around her uncle, but something about the way he looked at her changed in that moment. She was wearing her swimsuit, of course, but that shouldn't have mattered around family.

"Hi, Uncle Dave," she said, glancing down at her painted toenails...her mother had taken her to get a manicure and pedicure before she'd left on a trip with her best friend, leaving Gloria at home with her father and brother, which was fine.

Gloria had pretty much stayed out of his way, and he'd done the same for her, save when they had dinner together occasionally.

"You're going with your uncle today," her father informed her.

"Oh...okay," Gloria said, feeling more confused by the minute.

"Why don't you go put some clothes on?" her father suggested, going to get a beer for himself out of the refrigerator.

Gloria headed up the stairs to her bedroom. She ascended the wide staircase, and once she reached the top, she headed to the left, toward her wing of the family mansion.

Her father hadn't told Gloria where they were going, so she had no idea what to wear. She pulled on a pair of jean shorts and a tank top, then ran her fingers through her wavy blond hair before she put on some tennis shoes and headed back downstairs.

Uncle Dave had finished his beer, and he was waiting for her at the door, keys in his hand.

They had driven for about ten minutes, and Gloria could tell they were headed away from the city, out further into the country from where the estate was located.

"Horses?" Gloria asked.

"Do you like them?" her uncle repeated.

"Sure," Gloria replied. "Why do you ask?"

She'd ridden horses when she was in elementary school, and had done quite well, but when she'd started middle school she'd begun theatre, and hadn't had the time to commit to riding that she needed, so she'd made the decision to quit.

That had all been so long ago—at least to a child's mind—that Gloria hadn't thought about horses in ages, but she supposed that was how her uncle was choosing to relate to her.

"I thought I'd take you to a horse farm today, so you can see the horses."

"Oh. Okay."

Suddenly, he reached over and grabbed her hand, which shocked Gloria, making her gasp in surprise; if Uncle Dave had noticed, he didn't let on, as he held her hand. "It will be fun."

Gloria wasn't sure why he sounded menacing, but she told herself she was just being dramatic, that everything was fine.

That there was nothing weird about what was going on between her and her uncle...

They spent the afternoon looking at the horses, giving them treats, checking the farm out.

Gloria thought they were getting ready to go, but before they left, things with her Uncle Dave became even stranger.

"There's one more thing that I wanted to show you," he said, taking her hand again, in a way that made Gloria very uneasy.

"Uncle Dave, I should really be getting home—"

"Why, you have a curfew?" he asked, sounding amused. "Your Dad knows that you're with me. Come on."

Something in his tone let Gloria know she didn't have any other choice. She reluctantly allowed him to lead her down the barn aisle, past the tack room, to another door at the very end of the barn aisle.

He opened the door and held it open, motioning for her to go on in ahead of him.

"I don't—"

"Gloria, relax," he said, barely masking the impatience in his tone. "Everything is going to be okay."

She felt it in her gut, though, that everything was far from being anything close to ***okay****; Gloria had never been so uneasy in her life. Every instinct inside her told her to run, but she almost felt as though she were unable to move as her feet dragged her body inside the room.*

As soon as she stepped inside, Gloria saw that it was a small bedroom, likely for the barn help to sleep in. There was a bed against the far wall, underneath a window.

The sound of a lock clicking behind her caused Gloria to turn and see that her uncle had locked them inside the room.

Gloria caught her breath. "What's going on?"

"Trust me, sweetheart," he said, turning to face her.

Gloria backed across the room, afraid to turn her back on him.

He stared at her for a few more seconds, then slowly began crossing the room toward her.

Gloria gasped. "What are you doing?"

Her uncle acted as though he hadn't heard her. "You're becoming a beautiful young woman, Gloria. How old are you now?"

"F-fourteen," she stuttered, terrified.

"Very good. Do you have a boyfriend?"

"What does that have to do with anything?" Gloria asked, confused.

"Just answer the question, honey."

"Of course I don't."

"You're a good girl, aren't you?" Her uncle was standing right in front of her. Gloria could smell the beer on his breath as he leaned in, and she flinched as he stroked a strand of her blond hair. "You always were."

Gloria gasped as he leaned in and tried to kiss her. Gloria tried to push him away, but he grabbed her shoulders and held her in place.

“Relax, honey,” he said. “I’m just trying to show you some love.”

“I don’t—”

“You don’t want me to kiss you?”

He stared calmly at her, but Gloria could hear the unspoken threat in his tone.

She didn’t have a choice.

"Have you ever been kissed before, Gloria?"

She didn't answer. He held her face in his hand, lowering his own face until his eyes were level with hers. "Answer me, sweetheart."

"No," Gloria whispered.

"Just relax. It will be okay."

She moaned in protest as her uncle kissed her on the mouth in a most inappropriate way.

Gloria didn't dare move. Her body was clenched with tension as he kissed her, as his lips slobbered on hers.

He pulled back, kissing her cheek and taking her hand, leading her toward the bed.

Gloria dug her heels in. "Please, no."

"Gloria, honey, this is going to happen. I know you're a virgin, and that's good.

"That's why I wanted to give you this."

"Give me what?" she asked, her voice barely above a whisper.

"Your first time."

She felt tears welling in her eyes as he sat her on the bed, his arm around her waist as he held her close to him.

*Gloria had never been so terrified in her life. She didn't want him to **touch** her...she knew, however, that even if he let her go, she would never be the same again.*

And if he did what he said that he was going to do...Gloria knew she wouldn't survive it.

"Don't cry," he said, brushing a tear away. "If you relax, it won't be quite as painful."

"Why do you want to hurt me?" Gloria managed to ask, through her tears.

"I don't want to hurt you at all," he said, stroking her back. "I want to make love to you."

"No, please," Gloria begged, but he was already beginning to remove her clothes, unzipping her shorts.

"Lie back on the bed and relax. I promise you, the more you fight this, the more it's going to hurt."

"I don't want this. Stop."

He stood, unzipping his own pants. "This is happening, sweetheart. There's nothing you can do about it...so you may as well relax and try to enjoy it."

Gloria still remembered staring at the ceiling, how the beams were bare...she was staring again, although years later, thinking she'd escaped that particular realm of torture, that she'd never be raped again after she'd had her moment at her graduation party where she'd destroyed not only her pedophile uncle, but also her sorry-ass father, whose political career had been all but ended once Gloria confessed that he'd known what was happening and had allowed it to happen.

But she was being raped again. By the man who supposedly loved her...he was taking his anger out on her in the most vile, cruelest way imaginable.

And she didn't even have the strength to try to stop him.

Suddenly he was off her. While Gloria was still aching, the relief of no longer having him inside her was immense, enough that she finally succumbed to the darkness that had been at the edge of her vision that entire time...

"What the fuck do you think you're doing?" Mrs. Alexander demanded, hitting Henry hard as he was on top of her nearly unconscious daughter.

Henry immediately pulled out of Gloria. He was overcome with shame, and he grabbed the comforter and covered Gloria's naked lower half.

Mrs. Alexander had heard Henry's raised voice. She knew she shouldn't interfere, but when suddenly the yelling ceased and she heard the bed creaking, she feared the worst.

She'd never trusted Henry, and she'd heard his anger. The last thing she wanted was her daughter getting hurt.

But what she'd seen when she'd opened the door into the bedroom, she hadn't been prepared for.

Henry covered his wife because Gloria at least didn't deserve any more shame than he'd already given her, with her mother seeing her naked body after sex.

"Get away from her!" Mrs. Alexander shouted.

"I'm sorry—"

"Don't you fucking apologize! Don't you know what happened to her when she was a teenager?"

"Yes," Henry whispered, as he pulled his trousers back up.

"What the fuck is wrong with you! Get out!"

"I can't do that," Henry said. "She needs me."

"She needs you, hell!" Mrs. Alexander shouted. "You either get out of her house, or I'm calling the police. You'll never be able to hurt her again."

"I didn't mean to hurt her," he said. "I love her. She needs me to take care of her now—"

"What's wrong with you?" she repeated. "Leave. Now."

Henry knew he had no other options. He'd fucked up. He had ruined her life again...and his own. If his wife pressed charges, he knew he might never get to see their children again, and the idea of it terrified him, broke parts of him that hadn't already been broken by what he'd done to Gloria, by seeing her lying helplessly on the bed, unmoving, barely conscious.

Oh, fuck...what if he'd permanently damaged her...like, physically? And they'd been trying to have a baby...what if Gloria was already pregnant?

What if he had hurt their baby?

"Please let me stay," Henry begged, standing in the doorway of the bedroom, unable to look Mrs. Alexander in the eye.

"Get. Out," she growled, staring him down.

Henry turned, knowing he had no choice but to leave her, no matter how badly she needed him.

She needed aftercare. He needed to make sure she wasn't too badly hurt.

He was abandoning her.

He let himself out of the house with only his phone. He'd go to the pub, get a drink, and give things time to cool off before he called Gloria.

He knew no matter what he'd done to her she would forgive him, just as he'd forgive her for...well, it still hurt that she'd betrayed him, but not as badly as it hurt knowing what kind of a monster he was, having raped her. Henry had never done anything to a woman that she hadn't wanted him to do.

But his own wife, the mother of his children, he'd violated and violently assaulted.

He knew he would never forgive himself for what he had done; he could only pray Gloria would find it in her heart to forgive *him.*

"Sweetheart, are you okay?"

Gloria moaned, trying to move, trying to open her eyes, but it took too much effort. She wanted to lay still with her eyes closed. She wanted to sleep, because if she was asleep, she didn't have to face what had happened to her.

"Gloria," her mother said. "Gloria, open your eyes."

The urgency and fear in her mother's voice was the only thing to make Gloria leave the safe space of sleep.

She forced herself to look at her mother.

"Thank God," she said. "Oh, baby, I'm so sorry."

Gloria shook her head. "Don't—"

Her voice wouldn't come out as more than a whisper.

"Shh, he tried to strangle you. Don't speak."

"Mom, don't apologize. Don't worry about me..."

"Of course I'm going to worry about you."

"Where is he?"

Mrs. Alexander's face darkened. "I made him leave."

Gloria laid her head back on her pillow. "Oh."

"I think you need to go to the hospital."

"I'm fine. Please, no."

"Gloria—"

"Mom," she whispered. "Please. I can't face that. Just let me stay here."

"I'm afraid he hurt you—"

"I'm okay," Gloria whispered. "I promise."

She was already worried about what she was going to tell Eva, about why her Daddy wasn't at home, especially since he *had* been around lately. Gloria knew she had to be there for her daughters, no matter what she was going through. She was a mother, and that was the most important role that she would ever perform.

"Mom, what am I going to tell Eva?"

"Baby, don't worry about that right now—"

As if on cue, they both heard over the baby monitor that Eva had awakened, and she was leaving her bedroom, no doubt to come to her parents' room.

"Shit," Mrs. Alexander said. "I'll take care of her."

"No, she's my baby. Let her come to me."

"Sweetheart, you're half-dressed and, well, you've got bruises on your neck already."

"Give me my robe."

Mrs. Alexander grabbed Gloria's robe and helped her into it. Gloria was tying the robe closed around her waist as Eva came into the room.

"Mummy."

"Come here, baby," Gloria said, opening her arms for Eva to come to her.

She held Eva in her lap, flinching only slightly at Eva's weight on her pelvis, which was already aching and bruised from being forcibly held down.

"Mummy, where's Daddy?"

Gloria looked at her own mother to answer...after all, Mrs. Alexander was the one who had sent him away.

"He had to leave," Mrs. Alexander said.

"Will he be back tomorrow? I miss him," Eva said, burying her face against her mother's chest.

Gloria held her daughter close. "It will be okay, baby. I'm here."

"Can I sleep with you tonight?"

"You need to sleep in your own room, baby," Mrs. Alexander said.

"Please. Mummy?" Eva asked.

Mrs. Alexander knew Gloria couldn't tell Eva 'No,' but she also knew that her own daughter was in no shape to have Eva all night. Gloria needed to have some time to come to terms with what had happened to her.

"Baby, why don't we cuddle until you fall asleep," Gloria suggested. "Then we'll carry you to your own bedroom."

"Why can't I sleep with you?" Eva asked.

"Your Mummy is sick," Mrs. Alexander said.

Eva reached up to pat her mother's cheek. "I'm sorry you're sick, Mummy."

"It's okay, baby, I'll be fine," Gloria said, gently rocking Eva, despite the pain the movement caused in her bruised and beaten body. She hoped her pelvis was only bruised, not broken.

It only took ten minutes for Eva to fall asleep. Mrs. Alexander carried her back to her own bed while Gloria watched on the baby monitor, hating that she couldn't put her baby to bed herself.

Now that she was alone, she started to think about what had happened to her...about her betrayal of Henry, about her relationship with Dean being exposed, and about the horrible things her husband had said to her before he had raped her.

She tried to get to her feet. The pain between her legs was too intense. She wanted her phone. She knew her only chance to talk to Henry was while her mother was busy doing something else.

She tried again to stand, but it hurt too badly, reminding her so much of how she'd felt after that time in the barn, with her uncle...something she'd spent so much of her life trying not to think about, the years of therapy trying to relieve her mind of that trauma.

And the man whom she loved more than anything had forced her to relive it, and to experience that terrible pain, all over again...

Gloria was in tears when her mother returned to the bedroom.

"Oh, sweetheart," Mrs. Alexander soothed, sitting beside her daughter and gently wrapping her arms around her.

"I can't believe Henry would do that to me."

"I know. Baby...I was unable to save you from what your uncle did," Mrs. Alexander began, continuing to talk as she felt her daughter's entire body tense, "but I'm here now, and I won't let Henry hurt you, ever again."

"Mom...he's my husband."

"And he hurt you."

"I love him." Gloria looked at her mother. "I do. He didn't mean to hurt me."

"But he did," Mrs. Alexander said. "And there's no coming back from that. He *will* hurt you again. How many times has he hurt you in the past?"

"Never," she whispered. "Mom, I can't stand up, I'm too sore. Will you get me my phone?"

Gloria's mother wrapped her arms more tightly around her. "You don't need your phone; you don't need to talk to anyone."

Gloria met her mother's eyes as she said, "I'm calling my therapist."

11

Chapter Eleven

Mrs. Alexander picked up Gloria's phone. "How do I know you're not going to contact him?"

"You can stay with me." Gloria hesitated. "Or you could trust me."

Her mother gave her a long look, but handed Gloria's phone to her as she glanced down at the screen instinctively as Gloria's phone lit up with a new notification.

She looked down, then up at her daughter. "Gloria, who is Dean?"

Gloria swallowed. "Just give me my phone, please."

"How am I supposed to trust you if you don't tell me the truth?"

Gloria took a deep breath, then exhaled, defeated. "Dean is my boyfriend. Was, I mean. I broke up with him yesterday."

"Your boyfriend? You were having an affair."

"No. I mean, I've never met Dean, and he's never touched me. We haven't been sleeping together or anything like that."

Gloria wasn't in any shape to discuss Dean with her mother. Her feelings were still raw, even more so after what had happened with Henry.

"But you said he's your boyfriend."

"Was," Gloria repeated. "I ended things with him, because I love Henry."

Thinking about Henry set Gloria off, and for the first time since he had left, she burst into the kind of tears that felt they'd never end. She truly believed she was dying of sorrow.

"Gloria, please."

"I want him back," Gloria sobbed. "He's my husband. He's mine, and I'm his."

Mrs. Alexander sat on the bed beside her daughter. "Is this why he lost control of himself? He found out."

Gloria nodded. "When he picked up my laptop from getting repaired, he saw our messages." Gloria looked at her mother through her tears. "I swear, I was trying to break up with him before anything happened. I love Henry. But he was so sweet, and things between me and Henry are—were—far from perfect."

"Which is why I was here." Mrs. Alexander hugged her close. "I'm so sorry he hurt you, honey."

Gloria clung to her mother, burying her face in her shoulder. "I hurt him, too."

"There's no excuse for what he did to you. What you did was wrong, Gloria, and honestly, I couldn't blame him for leaving you...but he had no right to hurt you."

Gloria started sobbing harder. "No, I can't lose him!"

"I know it feels like you're dying right now, but you'll heal. You're still young, Gloria, and you've got three beautiful daughters. You *will* overcome this. You're the strongest person I know."

"No," Gloria said, pulling away and looking at her mother. "No, I hadn't left the house since the summer, before I took Briella shopping the other day. I'm a mess. I can barely function."

"How long has this been going on?"

Gloria shook her head. "I'm sorry, I need to speak to my therapist as soon as possible. I can't discuss this right now."

"Maybe we need to take you to the hospital," Mrs. Alexander said, "if you can't walk."

"And do *what* with the babies?" Gloria shook her head. "I'm okay. Can you give me a moment?"

Mrs. Alexander took her hand. "I'm not going to leave you right now."

Gloria's hand shook as she called and left a message with her therapist, telling her it was urgent.

As she was about to set her phone aside, she saw she was getting a call from Henry.

"I'm going to get you some water," Mrs. Alexander said. "Don't do anything rash, promise me." She kissed Gloria's forehead, then left the room.

Gloria stared down at her phone screen only for a moment, knowing she didn't have much time.

She felt sick as she took the call, her voice weak and tremulous as she said, "Henry?"

"Gloria. Baby. Fuck, I'm so sorry."

She bit down hard on her lip. "I'm not supposed to be talking to you. I only have a minute. My mother is in the kitchen."

"She won't let you talk to me."

"Do you blame her?" Gloria asked.

"Does she know that you cheated on me?"

"I wasn't cheating. But, yeah. She saw Dean calling me."

"Little cunt is still calling you?"

"I haven't spoken to him since I broke up with him."

"Gloria, that doesn't matter right now. Can I come home? We need to talk." He hesitated. "Baby, I am so, so sorry about what I did to you. I promise I'm not going to touch you."

"My mother will call the authorities if you step foot inside this house," Gloria said.

"Don't be a child. I'm your husband. We're supposed to work out our issues on our own. Your mother has no place interfering in our marriage."

"Just like rape has no place in a marriage, right, Henry? She's only trying to protect me."

"I won't hurt you. You know I won't ever do anything like that again, don't you? We've been together for years. Have I ever hurt you before today?"

"No. I want you to come home, but she's protecting me. I don't want you to end up in jail, okay?"

He sighed, deeply irritated. "Fine. Should I fucking go back up to Blackpool? What am I supposed to tell my children?"

"I suppose that's your business." Gloria heard her mother returning. "Henry, I've got to go. Fuck, I mean, I still love you."

"Prove it," he said. "Let me come home."

She bit back a sob as she ended the call, smashing her fist against her mouth to stifle her cries.

As soon as Mrs. Alexander walked into the room, she knew that something was wrong. "Gloria?"

"I'm fine," she whispered.

Giving Gloria a doubtful look, she sat on the edge of the bed, handing her a glass of water. "Here. And take this, too."

Mrs. Alexander handed Gloria two painkiller tablets, along with one of the pills Gloria had been prescribed for when she was having a severe panic attack.

"I don't need this," Gloria protested.

"You were just raped. Once it hits you, you'll need it. Go ahead and take it now. I can't handle seeing you have a severe attack tonight, Gloria." Mrs. Alexander shuddered. "I already had to see that monster on top of you, hurting you."

"Mom. Please."

"Think of how you'd feel if someone hurt Eva."

"Mom!"

"I'm sorry. You don't need that right now."

"No," Gloria cried, "I don't."

"Take the pills. I really want you to get a rape kit done at the hospital."

"I know Henry did it, Mom."

"You need evidence to put him away."

Startled, Gloria stared at her mother in disbelief. "I am *not* having my husband arrested. What would that do to our children? Besides," Gloria continued, "I need him here."

"He's never setting foot in this house again—"

"Mother, it's my house."

"And you're *my* daughter," Mrs. Alexander said. "You were mine long before you were ever his."

"And you let my uncle molest me for years. Your guilt over that is misplaced, trying to destroy my family."

Gloria knew she was being cruel, but she was desperate to keep Henry out of trouble. Even then, she knew he likely *did* deserve to go to prison. Gloria would have said so for any other man who had assaulted a woman. For heaven's sake, she'd just discussed it with Briella a few days before. Gloria was a grade A hypocrite, and she knew it...but she was so, so desperate to save her marriage.

No matter how he'd hurt her, she knew she needed him to function, to make it in the world. He had been her Dominant for years. He was a huge part of her identity, and so was their dynamic. Just the thought of navigating life, not only without Henry, but without their dynamic—which had been her source of belonging and comfort—was unbearable.

"I want to take a bath," Gloria said. "I think soaking and getting...it, off of me, would help me feel better."

"I don't like this, Gloria," Mrs. Alexander said, but she helped Gloria to her feet, carefully pulling her robe down to cover her pelvis and bruised thighs.

"I'm sorry for what I said, Mom." Gloria held her mother's gaze. "I didn't mean to bring it back up."

"I forgive you."

"Me, too, a long time ago." Again, Gloria hesitated. "Can I shower?"

"I suppose."

Gloria tried to walk, but the pain was still too great, not to mention she was feeling dizzy from being choked. "Do you think you can maybe help me?"

Mrs. Alexander wrapped her arm around her daughter's waist, helping her walk to the bathroom. She held Gloria up as she started the water and got the temperature right. "Can you do this on your own?"

Gloria nodded. "I'll hold onto the handrail, and I can sit if I need to." She held her mother's gaze for a moment. "Thank you."

"Of course. I'll change the sheets, then check on you, okay?"

Gloria nodded, waiting until her mother left the bathroom before she removed her robe, revealing her half-nude body.

She looked at herself in the mirror. The bruises were already forming, and she had scratches on her hips from where Henry had held her down and she'd struggled.

His cum was drying on her inner thighs, and she felt some still inside her, too.

She leaned against the glass door of the shower as she removed her shirt and bra, nearly breaking down when she saw the dark bruises already forming around her neck.

"Fuck, Henry. I know you were hurt, but you could have killed me," she whispered. "I think that's what you wanted, too."

She carefully stepped into the shower and reached for her shampoo, almost as though it were any other night, and she was showering before bed, like Henry would come in at any moment and get in with her...

She forced those thoughts down. She wanted to be able to wash his cum and sweat off before she broke down and cried like there was no tomorrow. She had tonight to mourn, then she had to have it together in the morning to be there for her daughters.

She might have betrayed her husband in some way, but she was never going to let her babies down, not for anything, and no matter the personal cost.

But by the time Gloria had her body wash and was gently working the creamy liquid into her skin, she reached between her legs to wash, and the pain was so intense she believed that she wouldn't survive it. If she couldn't even touch herself there with the gentlest of touches, how was she ever going to sleep with a man again?

She couldn't hold herself up any longer, allowing her legs to give out as she sank to her knees, letting the water wash over her, mingling with her tears, before even her knees gave out and she was lying on her painfully bruised hip, too exhausted and heartbroken to move into a more comfortable position.

Gloria curled onto a ball, wishing she could disappear, to escape the pain in her body *and* the intense pain shooting through her heart.

Henry was the first man to give her an orgasm, to make her feel safe again, to make sex pleasurable for her. Perhaps him being a dominant had taken the thinking part out of sex for her and having such rigid rules to abide by had made Gloria feel safe and protected. She allowed Henry to be in complete control of her, after all, and she did everything he asked. He'd always made her cum, and he'd even made her feel loved.

Gloria's heart felt as though it were literally breaking as sorrow flooded her entire body, and she let out a loud, ragged sob. Her weak body could no longer contain grief of the magnitude she was drowning in.

She wasn't sure how long she lay there on the tiled shower floor, literally writhing in agony—probably not all that long, but time had lost all sense of meaning—when the shower door opened and her mother stepped inside.

"My god, Gloria! Baby, what happened?"

Her mother had gotten into the shower, fully dressed as though it didn't matter to her that she was getting drenched. She only cared about her daughter—her own baby—and the pain she was in.

Gloria looked up at Mrs. Alexander. "I miss him so much."

"Shh, baby," her mother said, pulling Gloria in close to her, hugging her, stroking her wet hair. "I'm going to get you through this, okay? I promise."

Gloria loved her mother and loved her for the support she was giving her, but she knew Mrs. Alexander couldn't help her.

Only Henry could.

"Mom, I love him."

"I know."

"Please let him come home."

Her mother continued to hold her and stroke her hair. "Baby, stop. Just relax. Okay?"

"I need him," Gloria whispered...so softly that she wasn't even sure her mother had heard her.

After a while, the water got cold and Gloria was freezing. Mrs. Alexander had to have been just as cold, but she didn't complain as she shut off the shower and grabbed Gloria a warm towel, wrapping her up as though she were swaddling her, which only made Gloria cry harder.

She knew she didn't deserve her mother's love, especially not after she'd said the things she had earlier, and after she'd been unfaithful to her own husband.

"I know it doesn't seem like it right now," Mrs. Alexander said, "but it *will* get easier."

Gloria was too exhausted to keep talking. She leaned into her mother as Mrs. Alexander helped her into bed and into some pajamas.

"What did he do here?" she asked, touching Gloria's neck.

"Please," Gloria said, not at all in the mood to rehash what had happened with her and Henry...not then, and maybe not ever.

"How long has he been hurting you?"

"Mom," Gloria said, "before Henry, I was terrified of men. I didn't want to be touched. I never thought I'd be able to have a normal relationship with a man...I never thought I'd be able to have sex.

"He changed me. He taught me how to enjoy physical touch and how to not allow my trauma to keep me from enjoying sex with someone I want to be with.

"I don't know how to go on without him."

"And now that he's hurt you, do you really want to be with him, intimately, again?"

It was certainly a mother's intuition, as the second Gloria thought about Henry that way—even of him making love to her—she felt like she was going to suffocate.

"I know," Mrs. Alexander said, touching her daughter's shoulder comfortingly. "It's okay. You're safe now."

"I still love him."

"That will pass, too."

"Don't you still love Dad?"

Mrs. Alexander looked at her daughter for a long moment. "It's a little different."

"How so?" Gloria asked. "I'm married to Henry. We've got three children together."

"Your father and I have been together for ages, Gloria. And, on my own...I wouldn't have the money to leave him, even if I wanted to.

"You're not stuck. You don't depend upon Henry financially—"

"I'm dependent on him emotionally. That's even worse."

"You've never struggled for money. You had the family fortune, now you've got your own."

"I still feel as though you're trying to justify the fact that you never left Dad, and that you're using me as a poor example. Or living vicariously, perhaps. I'm not sure which."

"Gloria..."

"I'm sorry. I'm not trying to hurt you. I just need you to understand that my leaving Henry isn't easy."

"But you've got to."

Gloria glanced away, staring at a spot on the rug. She wondered if it was her blood, and that thought made her nauseated. "Do I, though?"

Eventually, Gloria fell asleep from sheer exhaustion; her mother had insisted upon sleeping in bed with her.

Gloria wondered if it was because Mrs. Alexander didn't trust her not to talk to Henry, or if it was because she feared Gloria might try to hurt herself.

Gloria had almost considered that possibility, but at the same time, she knew that her daughters were the ones giving her strength, keeping her there. She never wanted them to know what had happened, the kinds of things that their father was capable of.

Gloria hadn't even thought about the issue of whether she trusted Henry to see their daughters. She didn't have the slightest fear that he would ever hurt them, but she knew that her mother wouldn't allow it.

That, and Gloria hadn't thought him capable of what he'd done to her, either.

She'd formulated a plan, however, by the time her mother woke beside her, rubbing Gloria's back. "Are you awake, sweetheart?"

Gloria rolled over, flinching as pain overtook her entire body, soreness from the tension, her neck and throat hurting worse than she could have imagined possible, and between her legs felt like she'd been scraped with sandpaper and beaten with stones.

"Mom...I was wondering...I hate to ask this, but could I have the house to myself for a couple of hours this afternoon?"

"Why?" Mrs. Alexander asked, doubtfully.

Gloria hesitated. "My therapist got back with me this morning, early. She wanted to do a video session, and...I don't want the girls in the house when we discuss what happened."

Mrs. Alexander clearly wasn't happy about the idea, but she nodded. "Okay. As long as you promise me that you'll stay on the call with your therapist until I get home."

"Mom, you can't be my bodyguard forever, you know."

"You need me right now."

"So, do you agree?"

"As long as you do."

"Have a good time," Gloria said, kissing Eva as she handed her over to her mother, who had the twins in their stroller. She was taking them to the park just a block away from Gloria's building.

"I love you, Mummy."

"I love *you*, baby." Gloria looked at her mother. "Thank you for this."

"Just remember what I said. Call me if you need me. I'm just a block away."

"Okay."

Gloria waited about twenty minutes before she picked up her phone, fingers shaking as she dialed Henry.

"You can come now," she said, when he answered.

"Gloria, are you sure you're comfortable with me coming back to the house?"

"Should I not be comfortable with it?"

"I won't touch you, but I would understand if you're not okay with it."

"Please just come."

It was barely ten minutes before he entered the penthouse. Gloria was sitting on the sofa, covered in a blanket, curled into the corner against the armrest, hoping Henry would sit at the very least on the opposite end of the sofa. Just seeing him again filled her with fear.

"Baby."

She swallowed. "Have a seat."

He'd been making a move toward her, Gloria could tell, but he picked up on her demeanor and body language and kept his distance.

"How are you, babygirl?"

Gloria bit down on her lip, trying to keep herself from crying as she asked, "How do you think, Henry?"

"Baby, I am so sorry that I hurt you." He raked his hands through his hair. "I hate myself for it."

Gloria could tell he felt genuine remorse for having hurt her, but that didn't change the fact she was injured and traumatized, and that she was terrified of him.

He looked terrible, like he hadn't slept.

"Sit down," she repeated. "We need to talk."

"I will, Gloria, but I have to know, are you going to divorce me?"

"I don't know. I don't want to." She hesitated, searching herself for the words she needed to express what she needed to say, and to ask him for what she needed from *him.*

"Baby, please don't leave me."

"I thought I was so replaceable," she whispered, although she knew it was unfair to bring up things from their past.

"You're mine," Henry said.

"If that's the case, why did you have to rape me?" she asked, her voice breaking as she finally forced herself to meet his eyes.

Henry looked miserable. He took a step toward her, but she flinched away, and he immediately took two steps back.

"I am so, so sorry," he whispered.

"I'd feel more comfortable if you'd sit down," she said, nodding toward the opposite end of the sofa.

He gave her one last despairing look, then he took his seat, staring across the distance between them. "Babygirl. I love you more than anything. What I did was wrong, and I'm sorry. I promise you that I'll never hurt you again."

"I believe you," Gloria said, her voice barely a whisper.

"You do?"

"I believe that you believe what you're saying...I even trust that you won't hurt me again." She hesitated, wondering if she was putting her thoughts into words properly. "But I'm not sure that my mind believes what my heart knows to be true."

"What does that mean?" he asked.

"I'm never going to be comfortable with you again," Gloria whispered. "Every time you touch me, it's always going to be in the back of my mind...is he going to force himself on me again?"

Gloria suddenly realized the magnitude of what had happened to her. Her husband—the man whose responsibility it was to protect her, as he'd sworn to do—had hurt her in the worst way imaginable.

He'd taken her by force, and she was terribly injured. Her physical injuries would heal eventually, but that trust they had worked so hard to build, the trust that Gloria had depended upon, not only for her sanity, but also for her sense of identity, had been shattered.

She started crying again. Henry made a move toward her. She knew he only meant to comfort her, but the thought of him touching her again made her tremble, so he kept his distance. Gloria knew it was torturing him, not being able to help her when she was in so much pain.

As fucked up as the whole situation was, in that moment, Gloria realized just how much he must have truly loved her.

"Baby, I'll do anything. I swear. I'll make love to you exclusively...we never have to play our games ever again. I just can't lose you."

"I honestly can't even deal with the idea of the two of us being intimate. The thought of you touching me is enough to send me into a panic attack." She met his eyes, tears streaming down her face. "Fuck, Henry...I don't think we can fix this."

"Baby, don't say that, please," he begged. "No, I love you. You're my whole life, Gloria."

"Could you really forgive me for talking to another man?" she asked.

His expression darkened, and the look on his face reminded Gloria of how he had looked when he had attacked her. That unadulterated fury, even when it wasn't directed toward her, the thought that she could love a man capable of such anger scared her.

"Please," she said.

His expression softened when he realized that he was scaring her. "I'm sorry, babygirl. I mean...I'm sorry for everything."

"You...you never answered my question."

"I can forgive you."

"I guess you took it out on me, and now you feel better, right?" Gloria asked bitterly.

“I don’t know what you want me to say,” Henry began, raking his fingers through his hair. “I love you. More than my own life. I need you, every second of every day—"

“If that were true,” Gloria said, “then you wouldn’t have gone to the pub every night.”

He stared at her. “That’s not fair.”

Gloria looked down at her feet. “I know.”

“I love you.”

“Henry, I love you...but this, us? We’re broken beyond repair.”

“This is it, then?” he asked.

“I’m so sorry, baby.”

He put his face in his hands, sobbing. “I’ll do anything to fix this. Anything at all, baby.”

“You can’t fix it.”

“Gloria, don’t leave me. Don’t take my children from me.”

A sharp pang went through her chest. Did that mean Henry cared more about losing access to his children than he did about losing her?

Surely fucking not...

"Why would I stay in London? My whole life is in the States...other than you."

"I can't have my babies across the ocean." He swallowed hard. "Babygirl, I can't have you that far away from me."

He knew just what to say to reel her back in, too, which was why he was so dangerous.

"I'll spend the rest of our lives making it up to you."

"No, Henry. I've already made my mind up. I can't do this."

"Don't leave me," he whispered, looking up at her with tears streaming down his face.

Gloria stood, shaking in fear as she did so. But she knew she couldn't let Henry walk out of her life without comforting him in some way.

She sat beside him and wrapped her arms around him; when he started to hug her back, she flinched, and he stopped, letting her hold him as he sat perfectly still.

"I'll always love you, Henry, but I've got to leave you."

"Please," he begged, looking at her with a heartbroken expression on his face.

"I'm sorry."

He leaned his forehead against hers. That closeness and intimacy reminded her far too much of what he'd done to her the night before. "No, babygirl, I am the one who's sorry."

Gloria leaned up to kiss his cheek. "I love you. Goodbye, baby."

He tried to grab her hand as she stood, but Gloria refused to be pulled back into his snare, no matter how enticing the bait.

Henry was her weakness, and the only sustenance she'd ever thought that she would need.

"What about the children?" he asked, in a shaky voice.

"I could never take your children away from you," she said. "We'll discuss the details later...or maybe it's better if your lawyer discusses things with mine." She held his gaze. "Safer that way."

"You still believe I would hurt you again," he said, brokenly.

"I believe you could convince me not to leave you," she said, "and, baby, I can't risk that."

"Gloria."

"Henry," she said, turning from the doorway into the bedroom, where she was getting ready to lock herself until he left. "I love you. But this is over. You need to leave."

"Can't I get my things?"

She shook her head. "I can't be in this room with you."

She knew what would happen if he were in their bedroom with her. He would seduce her, and if that didn't work—if Gloria somehow managed to resist his charms—he would take what he wanted again, and he would make it impossible for her to kick him out.

"Gloria, I've got no clothes—"

"You've got money," she said. "Buy yourself some new clothes and stay in a hotel until you're able to leave for Blackpool. But you can't stay here a moment longer."

She turned her back on him then, stepping into the bedroom as she said, "Goodbye, Henry."

If he protested further, Gloria didn't hear him.

She locked the door, then grabbed a blanket off her bed and retreated into her closet, locking that door as well.

It was the only way she knew to keep from running back to her husband and begging him to stay.

Gloria knew her mother would be home soon enough. Mrs. Alexander would help her plan her move back to the U.S., and she would protect her daughter—and her granddaughters—no matter the cost.

She also knew that—if Henry turned vindictive and decided to try to take her babies—that her father's lawyers would eat Henry alive, no matter how strained the relationship between Gloria and her father.

Mr. Alexander never would have missed an opportunity to prove his power.

She prayed it didn't come to that. She didn't want to hurt Henry.

It would kill her if she had to keep the babies from him.

Gloria was going to have to rely on the protection of the family that had turned their backs on her, and she was having to walk away from the only man that had ever made her feel safe.

And—somehow—Gloria was going to have to figure out how to survive in the world as a submissive without her dominant.

TO BE CONTINUED

ACKNOWLEDGEMENTS

First, I want to thank my mother for being my number-one supporter from the beginning.

Thank you to my family for supporting me, my writing, for reading my books, and for giving me feedback.

Finally, I want to thank my friends from the online writing community. You all have offered me an unbelievable amount of support and love, have taught me so much, and I am eternally grateful for your support from day one, and for encouraging me to keep going. You're all the reason why this is all possible. Specifically, I want to thank author Daria M Paus for her help with this book. You are a kind and generous soul and I'm forever grateful for your help!

Thank you for reading my book. I will continue to write and publish books for you all for years to come.

Sneak Peek of The Dirt Bike Rivals: Jenny's Story

Chapter One

Jennifer Miller carried the stack of files tightly against her chest, pressed into her belly button and also into her chin as she made her way up the steep stairs of her office in her stilettos. As the youngest junior executive at her firm, she did what was asked of her, and she did so in style.

No matter how much more difficult her fashion choices made it to do her job, Jenny always did so in style, and—despite what any of her friends suggested—her wardrobe had nothing to do with her sexy-as-hell boss, the CEO of Grainger Outfitters, a multi-billion dollar outdoors and sporting goods company. Jenny always thought it was funny that Edward Novik was the CEO of a sporting goods company...she could never imagine him being anything other than the ultra-serious, buttoned-up man who made sure that she towed the line nonstop at work...something that still didn't sit right with Jenny, considering that she seemed to be the only one in her department who received that kind of treatment from him, as he was down-to-earth and kind to everyone else...which was simply one more thing that frustrated Jenny deeply, along with the sexual desires she felt for him, that she quashed with ferocity.

The thing that was really killing Jenny's buzz that morning was the fact that she had come into work hot from the dream she'd been having, right before her alarm went off. She had been summoned to Edward's office in her dream, uneasily expecting the worst. It was likely she'd left a comma off an email, or that she'd had the wrong type of staples ordered for his office, but he was ready to fire her over it, she assumed.

Then she had walked into the office, and he'd been sitting behind his desk, glowering at her.

She'd taken a deep breath. "Mr. Novik, whatever I did, I'm sorry—"

"Don't speak, Jennifer."

In her dream, she had swallowed and closed her mouth.

"I want to see you swallow, Jenny, but don't you open your mouth unless it's to wrap your lips around me."

Jenny had groaned loudly when her alarm going off had ruined the blow job she'd been giving her boss...and she'd almost been late for work, having had to take care of a couple of things before she'd been able to drag herself out of bed that morning...and she had a nagging feeling that Edward knew she'd been late.

He had summoned her to his office after she'd only been at work for half an hour, barely long enough to secure her schedule for the day and to finish her first cup of coffee. Her best work friend, Maggie, had been the one to stick her head into Jenny's immaculate office. "Girl, Mister Sexy Pants wants to see you."

"Pardon?"

Maggie smiled. "You know."

Jenny's face paled. "How does he know everything that goes on here?!"

"It's kind of his job...being CEO and everything."

"Running my life isn't his job."

"Do you think it has anything to do with the fact that your parking spot is in his direct line of vision of his office?"

Jenny scowled.

"Just stating the obvious," Maggie said, in her pencil skirt, silk blouse, and silky brown hair.

Jenny grabbed her tablet and set her jaw, heading up the stairs to see her boss.

Her knees shook a little as she walked to his office and timidly tapped on its door.

She heard laughter coming from inside, and moments later the door opened and Misty Waters stepped out of Edward's office.

While Jenny dressed like a boss, Misty dressed like she wanted Edward's attention...and it looked like she was getting it.

It pissed Jenny off that she was irritated by Misty's presence in her boss' office...especially since Jenny was supposedly in trouble, and the last thing that she wanted was to be alone with him if she were in trouble. Having Misty as a buffer would have been preferable, despite the fact that she wasn't a huge fan of her coworker.

Misty smiled knowingly at her. "Oh, hello, Jennifer."

"Hello, Misty." Jenny forced herself to smile back at the woman.

Misty smirked at her, then turned back around to face Edward. "Mr. Novik."

"Thank you, Miss Waters."

Jenny tried not to breathe in as Misty walked past her, exiting Edward's office...trying to avoid the smell of Misty's perfume.

Once the air had cleared somewhat, Jenny took a deep breath and stepped into Edward's office. Her knees were still shaking, but she clenched her buttcheeks together to try to keep it from being obvious...especially as her stomach started to cramp a bit with nerves.

She swallowed. "You wanted to see me, Mr. Novik?"

"Yes. Please come in, Miss Miller."

She took another small step into the room.

He glanced up from his desk. "Close the door."

Jenny felt her eyes widen, but she did as he'd told her, closing the door behind her, standing just inside it, afraid to come all the way inside his office, because she knew what was coming...the same thing that had been coming every time that she had gone up to his office for the past three weeks or so, since he had apparently decided that she was a slack-off who couldn't be trusted.

"Um...Mr. Novik, I wanted to apologize—"

"You could begin with apologizing for what you just said."

She took a deep breath. "Um, for what?"

He stared at her. "Think about it."

She bit her lip, and the furrow in his brow seemed to deepen.

"I'm sorry, Mr. Novik."

"For what?"

"For...saying 'um,'" she said, quickly realizing her mistake.

It had gotten worse over the past few weeks. Criticizing her for saying 'um'? When he was so chummy with Misty, who worked half as hard as Jenny did?

"Miss Miller, you know that I have high expectations of those whom I employ, correct?"

"Yes, Mr. Novik."

"I also expect my employees to arrive at work *on time.*"

"Mr. Novik, I—"

"You were late for work, weren't you?"

She chewed on her lip again, and her boss stood up. "I suggest you arrive at work on time from now on. Employee reviews are to be updated soon. I would hate to have to leave you anything negative."

She flinched. "I'm sorry, sir."

"I want you to enjoy working here. Do you enjoy your job?" he asked.

"Yes, sir."

"Okay." He looked back down at his desk. "That's all I needed, Jennifer. Have a nice day."

She frowned, staring at him, although he didn't look up from his computer again.

"Um, you too, Mr. Novik."

He glared up at her, and she flinched.

"I mean, I apologize. Have a nice weekend, Mr. Novik."

Jenny was in such a hurry to get out of her boss' office that she didn't even notice that he had called her 'Jennifer' until she sat back down at her desk, reaching for her now cold cup of coffee...

Chapter Two

"He made you apologize for saying 'um'?" Maggie asked, incredulous.

It was much later in the day, after work. Maggie, Jenny, and some of the other women in the office had decided to start their weekend off with after-work drinks at CeeCee's, a bar that was popular with the professional crowd, and was an especially popular hangout on Friday evenings.

Jenny had been fuming all day, but like any professional, she had kept her anger in check and hadn't said anything to anyone about her visit to their boss' office. Even on their lunch break, she'd been tight-lipped and—admittingly—moody, but she hadn't stopped for one moment being the perfect professional. She'd worked even more meticulously all day, for fear of upsetting Edward.

She hated to admit that she was afraid of her boss.

But what Jenny hated even more was that it turned her on, being afraid of him...

She'd even started worrying that she was subconsciously getting into trouble so that she could get called to his office...some sick game she'd been playing that she didn't even know about.

"Yes."

Jenny wasn't as angry as she had been before, though...the more she thought about it, the more she only wanted to forget about what had happened. She was a professional, and she could do better. She would start showing up early for work if she had to.

She would do whatever she had to do.

At that moment, though, all that Jenny wanted to do was to have a drink and to try to relax, not to have to think about work, or her boss...or the fact that he'd called her 'Jennifer.'

"I don't get it, why does he have it out for you?" Maggie asked. "He's always been nice to me, even complimenting the last report I wrote for him."

"I don't know." Jenny took another long sip of her Jack and Coke.

"He's sweet to *me,*" Misty said. "Always has been."

Jenny drained her drink. "I need another."

"I'll come with," Maggie said, and the two women got up and approached the bar, leaving the rest of their friends—and Misty—as they went in search of fresh drinks.

"Misty is such a little—"

"She wears cheap perfume, give her a break," Jenny said.

Maggie laughed, then prepared to order her a new drink as a man a few seats down came up between the two women and put his arm around Maggie's shoulders. "These drinks are on me," he told the bartender, who nodded.

"In that case, I'll have a redheaded slut," Maggie said.

Jenny stifled a laugh, but the man was far from deterred. Instead, he wrapped his other arm around Jenny's shoulders. "Sounds good to me."

"I've heard that one before," Jenny retorted, ordering another Jack and Coke.

"Can't blame me for trying, darling," the man said.

Jenny shrugged. "Thanks for the drink."

"No problem, princess."

Jenny and Maggie walked back to their friends with their drinks. Jenny rolled her eyes. "He was kind of cute."

"Well, I'm sure that he would love to rock your world tonight, 'princess,'" Maggie retorted.

Jenny laughed, and it felt good...maybe Maggie was right. It had been a long time since her last boyfriend, and it would certainly be good stress relief from her job...

They sat back down at the booth with their friends, and Jenny wasn't remotely surprised to note that Misty was still talking about her favorite fantasy, which was the day that their boss, Mister Edward Novik, would decide that he was in love with her, that he would ask her for her hand in marriage and that she would be a wealthy housewife from that day forward.

Jenny had heard that story too many times, and the mention of her boss was turning her stomach worse than her third Jack and Coke was. The last thing that she wanted to spend her weekend doing was thinking about Edward Novik, her job, or anything work related.

In fact, that gentleman from the bar was looking more and more attractive...

But she wasn't desperate. She would keep making eyes at him, and if he approached their table, she would make her move.

"I know he wants me," Misty sighed. "He kept staring at my chest today in his office."

"Are you sure that there just wasn't anything else to look at?" Maggie asked innocently, winking at Jenny when Misty looked away.

Jenny stifled a laugh.

"Yes, I'm sure," Misty said. "And you'll all be laughing when I'm Mrs. Novik and I get my husband to fire you hoes."

"Please don't," Jenny said.

"No worries, dear, I'm sure you won't last that long." Misty perked up, then. "What were you called in for, anyway?"

"None of your business," Jenny said, not sure why she was being so sensitive about it.

"Whatever it was, just be grateful that I put him in a better mood before you came in," Misty said, rolling her eyes.

Jenny took that as her cue. She stood and headed for the bar...she didn't need any more alcohol, but she *was* still thirsty...and she still wanted to talk to the hot bar guy, although she knew it was a mistake.

But she did seem to be making an awful lot of those, as of late.

She approached the bar, where the man was still sitting. She sat beside him, leaning across the bar. "Just a coke this time, no Jack."

"Why not, princess?" the guy asked.

Jenny smiled at him. "It's been a long day."

"So why not indulge, relax a little?"

"I've already had three." She shrugged.

"So, you looking for another kind of stress relief, baby?"

"What did you have in mind?"

The guy leaned in, his lips almost grazing her neck as he said, "Come back to my place, sweetheart, and I'll make you forget everything else."

"Tempting. I don't sleep with strangers, though," Jenny said.

"Then let's not be strangers. I'm Daniel."

Jenny laughed. "Daniel."

"And you are?"

But before Jenny could answer, another man placed himself between her and Daniel. "She's not interested."

Jenny frowned...and when the man turned around, she froze.

Edward Novik.

She stood, backing away from the bar. "Mr. Novik?"

"Miss Miller."

"Um...sorry, is this some roleplay thing?" Daniel asked.

"No, he's my boss," Jenny said, backing away from the bar. "And I'm leaving."

But by the time Jenny had made her way to the exit and was putting on her coat, her boss was standing in front of her. "Miss Miller—"

"I'm your employee," she said. "Not your property."

His brow furrowed in a similar way to how it had when she'd been in his office earlier that morning. "Miss Miller, I'm well aware of our relationship. I was only looking out for you, as a man should protect a woman he knows."

"Looking out for me?" she demanded, in disbelief.

He nodded. "That's what I said, Jennifer."

She buttoned her coat. "Good night, Mr. Novik."

"Jennifer, wait."

She frowned, but she turned to look at him.

"I know Mr. Simpson."

"Who?" she demanded.

He grimaced. "Daniel. The man who propositioned you at the bar."

She laughed. "I believe I was propositioning him."

"He's not a good man."

"Why do you care, Edward?!"

"Because you're my employee, and I want my employees to be viable workers, which they can't be if they're heartbroken over a bastard who takes advantage of vulnerable women!"

"I'm not a vulnerable woman," Jenny insisted. "You don't know me at all."

"Well," he said, softly, "maybe I'd like to know you, Jennifer."

She bit her lip. He leaned in, towering over her, and she swallowed hard…remembering what he'd said to her in her dream that morning.

She closed her eyes, not sure what she was expecting to happen…but then, he whispered into her ear, "Good night, Miss Miller. Don't be late for work Monday morning."

Jenny's eyes shot open, but by then, Edward Novik was gone.

She glanced around the dark bar, then stepped outside, but it was like he'd vanished into thin air.

In a panic, Jenny realized that she'd called him 'Edward…'

Shit, she thought.

But then someone grabbed her arm. She turned, expecting to see her boss, but it was Daniel.

"Oh. Daniel, I'm so sorry about what just happened…"

"You know Novik?" he asked.

"I mean. He's my boss."

"Oh." Daniel nodded.

"Yeah. So, how do you know him?" she asked.

"Long story." He hesitated. "Do you want to come back to my place?"

She sighed…with everything that had happened, her horniness had dissipated somewhat. She was fuming over her boss trying to control her personal life, and she was nervous that she'd lost her temper and that she'd called him 'Edward.'

"I mean, we don't have to do anything, princess. We can just talk."

She laughed. "Sure."

"No. Jenny. I can tell you're upset. And to be frank, it's clear that Edward wants you for himself, and I'm not looking to make more of an enemy of him than I already have, so—"

"Enemy?" Jenny asked.

Daniel sighed. "Just follow me back to my place?"

She exhaled, deeply. "Fine."

Daniel smiled, but then he winked at her. "Don't sound so excited, baby."

She shook her head, but laughed.

Daniel truly was funny.

"Okay, Daniel," she said.

"Come on."

He took her hand and walked her to her car, then she got in. He told her his address, and he left her to go get into his car.

Chapter Three

Jenny ignored the missed calls on her cell phone as she followed Daniel into his apartment. He lived in a nice part of town, not too far from where Jenny worked, and it wasn't hard to find at all...which was good for a variety of reasons.

First of all because she was insanely curious about what Daniel knew about her boss...but also because she'd realized just how hot Daniel truly was, and she was even more frustrated than she had been before Edward had intercepted, and she had every intention of defying his wishes and getting a little relief from how stressed she'd been from work.

She wanted to sleep with Daniel.

He wrapped his arm around her waist as he escorted her up the stairs to his apartment. They didn't talk, but he stopped to cup her cheek in his hand, to brush his lips against hers...he was romantic and sweet...or, she supposed, as romantic as a hookup from a bar could be.

He unlocked the door to his apartment. "After you, princess."

She smiled at him, stepping into his apartment. He flicked on the lights, and she turned to face him as he closed the door behind them.

She saw the look in his eyes, and he closed the distance between the two of them, taking her face in his hands and kissing her.

Jenny sighed as she felt his soft lips against hers, and his gentle fingers stroking her face and running through her hair.

He took off his shirt and she briefly admired his muscled chest and arms before she felt his hands on her waist...lifting her blouse, untucking it from her skirt.

"No, wait," she protested.

He sighed. "Sorry."

She wrapped her arms around him, stifling a moan at the feel of his solid form against her body. "No, I just want to talk first."

"Anything you want, princess," Daniel said, softly.

He took her hand and led her from his foyer, across his brick floor, to the huge leather sofa in his living room.

His apartment was sparse but nice, with brick walls as well as the floors, and was decorated in a minimalistic style, but in a way that Jenny could tell that he had money.

She turned to look at him. "What do you do for a living, Daniel?"

"I'm the CEO of a successful outdoor and sporting goods company. One that's direct competition to the one that Edward Novik runs, and that you work for."

She took a deep breath. "No wonder he doesn't want me to sleep with you."

Daniel frowned. "Did he say that?"

Jenny shrugged.

"Jennifer," he said, "listen, whatever he said, it's not true."

"I don't know what to think. But it pisses me off that he thinks he can tell me who to date."

"Date?"

Jenny looked at him, raising her eyebrows.

"So, you know why he's my enemy then."

"And I can understand why he doesn't want his employee to sleep with the CEO of a rival company," Jenny said.

"And do you care?"

She winked at him.

Daniel smiled, wrapping his arms around her, pulling her close. Jenny sighed, completely content. Daniel was so sexy, and he was so good at kissing her and touching her...

She moaned softly as Daniel eased his tongue between her lips, his hand working its way down her back, as he held her waist firmly, pulling her closer. Jenny knew how it worked, how hookups went. She was a grown woman and she'd had a number of boyfriends...after her last one had cheated on her, though, Jenny had kind of given up on the whole institution of dating. She'd lived like a nun for months, then she'd started going for drinks with Maggie, and she'd found that bars were an endless source of men wanting to buy her a drink...and to get whatever else they could get, too.

So whenever she had a dry spell lasting more than a few months, she decided to test the waters, and it seemed she'd hit the jackpot with Daniel. She felt that fact doubly when she shifted closer to him and felt his erection pressing against her as he gathered her into his lap. She sighed, looking down into his lust-filled gaze as he ate her alive with his eyes.

"You're so sexy, Jennifer."

She thought back to when she'd been in her boss' office earlier that day, when he'd let it slip and had called her 'Jennifer.'

"Call me 'Jenny,'" she said, moving her lips to his neck, kissing and sucking.

He moaned, grabbing her face in his hands and pressing his lips against hers. She ran her hands down his chest, feeling his muscles through his shirt.

"You're not built like a guy who works all the time," she said, running her hands over his chest, down to his shirt tail, where she began undoing his buttons, revealing his solid, hairy chest...she was always a sucker for men with ample body hair, and the more she revealed of Daniel's chest, the hotter he was.

"I have a gym at my office, princess."

She began working the zipper on his trousers. "Nice."

He laughed, tangling his fingers in her hair as she got on her knees in front of him.

"You don't waste any time, do you, baby?"

She smiled up at him, easing down his pants, down to his knees...she really wasn't in the mood to wait, but she grabbed her handbag and dug out a condom.

He grabbed her hair as she lowered her head between his legs. She yanked down his boxers—so he was a boxer man, not briefs—and she quickly eased the condom over his length.

He was nice and hairy, which she'd expected, and it made her panties wet, looking at his well-endowed self as she prepared to take him in her mouth.

She took his thick length in her hands, rubbing her thumbs over his veiny shaft sheathed in latex. She was so eager to wrap her lips around him that she was salivating.

"Like what you see, princess?"

"Yes, I do."

She grabbed him hard, pressing her thumb against the underside of his head, rubbing that spot that she knew drove men wild, as she looked up into his eyes and ran her tongue along his length.

He groaned, twisting his fingers through her fiery curls, getting a firm grip as she wrapped her lips around his dick, quickly moving her head up and down over his length, flooding her panties as she sucked him hard, taking him deep so that he hit the back of her throat.

Despite the fact that Jenny had her fair share of practice with giving head, she still cringed at her gag reflex, but Daniel didn't seem to mind as he guided her head over him, flexing his hips so that he pressed deeper into her mouth, increasing the pace at which he thrust as she bobbed her head faster, working her tongue over him, tightening her lips around him as she sucked him off.

She gently raked her nails across his balls, feeling them tighten as he prepared to cum into her mouth...or, into the condom she'd slipped over his large cock.

He held her hair tightly, his dick shoved deep into her throat as he came.

Jenny whimpered around the large cock she had shoved down her throat. She swallowed gently, and he finally eased his grip on her hair, taking her face tenderly in his hands.

He smiled down at her. "You're beautiful, Jenny."

"Then kiss me."

He leaned down and pressed his lips against hers; Jenny moaned, opening her mouth as he slipped his tongue in...there was something erotic about a man who tongue kissed after his dick had been in her mouth...she loved it.

"Damn, Jenny."

She whimpered as he pulled away. He leaned back, staring down at her like she was the hottest woman in the world.

"No need to fret, princess."

He stood abruptly, but moved carefully around her. She watched him as he walked around his sofa, into the kitchen. She watched him kick open the trash compactor and listened as something hit the bottom of the can...his condom, she figured, as he came back and was unsheathed, but she watched with rapt interest as he hardened before her eyes, seeing her still on her knees, watching him with her big blue eyes.

Daniel crossed the room and was before her in moments. He held his hands out to her, and she took them...he helped her to her feet, brushing her hair back from her face.

Jenny was shocked by how romantic he was, and how tenderly he touched her. She shifted uncomfortably as her panties stuck to her.

Daniel ran his hands down to her butt, cupping her cheeks through her skirt as he gave them a hard squeeze...the harsh grip of his heavy hands on her ass contrasted with the softness of his lips on hers made her even drippier and needier.

She gasped for air when their lips parted. She looked up, meeting his eyes.

"What do you need, sweetheart?"

She bit her lip. "You. I need you."

He reached down and swiftly began unbuttoning her shirt. She gasped as she felt his surprisingly rough hands against the sensitive flesh of her belly. She sucked in her breath, then she pressed against him as he took her shirt off and cupped his hands over her breasts, over the silk of her bra. He kissed her neck, licking and nipping as he unzipped her skirt and pushed it off her hips, so that she stood before him in her lingerie and her heels.

He grabbed her hips hard. "I want you, Jenny."

"Then take me."

He smiled down at her for a few moments...then before Jenny knew what was happening, he had her over his shoulder, carrying her to his bedroom.

Jenny gasped, then laughed, but then he grabbed her butt hard, squeezing her naked cheek that he had easy access to, since she wore a thong.

She softly moaned, biting down hard on her lip...she was betting that he was a real freak in bed, and she was eager to find out just how much of one her new lover was, and what his kinks and limits were.

He shoved open the door to his bedroom...she hadn't really noticed much else about his apartment, as she was mostly focused on how strong he was, and her libido was ridiculously high and she was nearly crazy with horniness.

However, Jenny forced herself to rein in her pussy as she raised up on Daniel's shoulders and looked at the interior of Daniel's bedroom...he had no visible torture devices, and he didn't have boxes of pizza and cans of beer strewn across his room, so that wasn't too bad, she supposed.

At the same time, she scanned for any items of clothing perhaps belonging to a girlfriend or wife he was hiding, and saw nothing at first glance. She'd learned that you could never be too careful when it came to sizing up lovers she hooked up with at bars, you never knew what you were getting.

Daniel lay her carefully across his bed, then knocked the pillows and comforter to the floor as he crawled into his bed with her, pushing her thighs apart.

She gasped, then lifted her hands above her head, grabbing the pillow and clenching it in her hands...she could tell from the way that Daniel was looking at her that it was going to be a rough ride, and she couldn't wait.

Daniel smiled at her then, the predatory look gone from his face. He could switch back and forth so fast that it made her spine tingle...but she wanted to be ravished by the roguish man, not the joker.

"You're lovely. I could just feast on you with my eyes all night, princess."

She smiled back, then slowly spread her thighs, arching her back slightly as she subtly moved closer to his face. She saw his eyes slip down, feasting on the damp patch of silk right between her legs, her sweet spot that was leaking honey for him to lap up.

He moaned, and that devilish look came back to his eyes. "But I think I need a taste, sweetheart."

"I want you to taste."

He grabbed her thighs and pulled her down to him. She gasped when she felt his fingers brush against her sensitive spot, and flinched when he tugged her panties aside...but then she felt his fingers rubbing her, and she pushed back against him, right into his touch.

He moaned as loudly as she did, as his fingers slipped right inside her, as she opened her thighs and began riding his hand, insisting on more.

He let her play some more before he pulled his hand out of her pussy. He moved back up the bed, brushing his nude body against hers as he settled himself beside her, wrapping an arm around her waist and pulling her close.

He grabbed her face in one hand, and pressed his wet fingers of his other hand against her lips, which she promptly opened, licking and sucking her cum off of him until his fingers were clean.

Then he kissed her again.

"You're so hot, Jenny," he said, reaching behind her to unclasp her bra.

She whimpered as the cool air hit her bare skin...then she was whimpering and moaned for an entirely different reason, as Daniel sucked her nipples and licked her breasts.

"More," she whispered.

"Be careful what you ask for, princess."

Seconds later, he had pulled her into his lap, so that she was straddling him. She felt his massive erection against her wet silk panties, and she groaned, but placed her hand against his chest.

"What's wrong?"

"Condom."

He kissed her cheek, then he reached back to grab at his bedside table, where he withdrew a foil wrapper and quickly slipped it on his hard cock. She grabbed his arms and positioned herself on top of him again, and he pushed her panties aside as he nudged at her dripping opening with the head of his cock.

Jenny spread her thighs wide as she braced herself against Daniel's shoulders for the impact of his penetration. The slight discomfort from the condom sucking at her dampness was quickly forgotten as he pushed all the way inside her, making her moan.

He wasted no time, as soon as he'd pushed all the way inside her, he began thrusting hard up inside her.

She held tightly onto his shoulders as she found his rhythm and began to match it, moving her tight little body in time with his, meeting his thrusts, grinding the inside of her pussy against the head of his cock, hitting that spot that made her whole body shake.

She was glad that Daniel wanted it hot, fast and heavy, as she didn't think that she could hold out long before she started clenching around his thick cock.

He shifted her, grabbing her hips hard and shoving in deep, hitting her g-spot over and over...

"Daniel," she gasped.

"It's okay, baby, come for me."

She moaned loudly, then screamed as he pushed in one last time, deeper than ever. He started shaking, and he buried his face against her shoulder as he came, as Jenny's pussy pulsed around him.

Finally, when they'd both settled down some, he pulled out and laid her back across his bed. He leaned over her and licked and kissed her breasts again, making her feel that eager stir inside her now dirty panties, and in her belly...like her appetite for this man could not be satiated.

He made glorious little sucking sounds as he kissed and lapped at her breasts and her soft pink nipples, making her whimper as she reached up to work her fingers through his thick brown hair.

"I already want you again, Jenny."

She moaned, throwing her head back against the pillows. "Then take me. I'm yours, baby."

He laughed, and she shivered at the feel of the rumble in his chest as his body pressed against hers. He met her eyes, and she knew he felt the same thing that she did...an insatiable hunger that neither of them would ever satisfy.

"Jenny, I want you to be mine," Daniel said, taking her face in his hands.

"What do you mean?"

"I know we just met, but I don't want this to end tonight. I want to see you again."

She sighed.

"I can tell you don't like the idea of that."

She shook her head, stroking his hair. "It's not that. I want to keep sleeping with you, but I don't want a boyfriend."

"Jenny...I don't like the idea of you being with other men."

She frowned.

"I don't want you to talk to anyone else."

"That doesn't sound possessive and controlling at all."

"No, you don't get it, Jennifer."

She grabbed his shoulders and pulled him down against her. "I'm Jennifer, now?"

"I just...I'm not great with talking."

She laughed, then her lips found his...all she wanted in that moment was him, and he was there, hers for the taking.

She would worry about the rest in the morning, she supposed.

He mumbled something incohesive against her mouth, and they just kept kissing. His fingers found her most sensitive spot, and he started to play with her, making fire burn between her legs and deep in her belly.

"I think you need to lose these," he said, and Jenny was barely aware of what Daniel was doing as he pulled off her panties and tossed them aside.

He leaned back over her, kissing her as he slipped his fingers into her sweet wetness, then he whispered, "I like the thong. I want you to wear those for me, okay, princess?"

"Hmm. As long as I'm in the mood," Jenny retorted, smirking up at him.

He kissed her again. "You'll be the end of me, baby."

Jenny simply wrapped her legs around him and pulled his huge, hard body down on top of her...she wasn't done with him, yet.

If you enjoyed this excerpt and would like to read more of Jenny's story, as well as Maggie and Misty's stories, the entire Dirt Bike Rivals series is available on Amazon's Kindle store!

Also, if you enjoyed Duplicitous and would like to support me as an author, I would greatly appreciate it if you would leave an honest review. Reviews mean everything to authors! Thank you!

About the Author

Teffeteller has been writing her whole life, deciding she wanted to become a novelist after a) receiving a "not college ready" score on her state writing assessment in high school, and b) one of her high school English teachers telling her she was a terrible writer.

Years later, after earning an honors degree in English from a challenging state university, and publishing over eighteen books under various pen names, Teffeteller is glad that she followed her dreams instead of the doubts of others.

Teffeteller fell in love with romance novels at age eighteen, the summer before she started college and found a random Harlequin romance novel at her local discount thrift store...from that point forward, she couldn't get enough. Her favorite romance authors are Stephenie Meyer, Pat Booth, and Rebecca Bloom, among many others.

When she isn't writing, Teffeteller enjoys reading Wattpad, watching Netflix, or the Gossip Girl reboot on HBO, shopping, and working out.

She loves both the mountains and the beach, which is why Santa Monica is the most perfect place on earth.

Also By

The Winter Suites Series

Lipstick and Heartbreak, Vol. 1

What Happened in Reno, Vol. 2

The Burtonelli Siblings Series

Her Innocent's Reckoning

The Family Affair

The Noble Assassin

Catharsis duet

Absolution, Book One

Duplicitous, Book Two

The Dirt Bike Rivals Series

Jenny's Story

Maggie's Story

Misty's Story

Milton Keynes UK
Ingram Content Group UK Ltd.
UKHW020918050424
440683UK00004B/213

9 798224 066995